THE COUNTRY BRIDE

BY
DIANNE DRAKE

All the characters in this book have no existence outside the imagination of the author, and have no relation whatsoever to anyone bearing the same name or names. They are not even distantly inspired by any individual known or unknown to the author, and all the incidents are pure invention.

All Rights Reserved including the right of reproduction in whole or in part in any form. This edition is published by arrangement with Harlequin Enterprises II B.V. The text of this publication or any part thereof may not be reproduced or transmitted in any form or by any means, electronic or mechanical, including photocopying, recording, storage in an information retrieval system, or otherwise, without the written permission of the publisher.

MILLS & BOON and MILLS & BOON with the Rose Device are registered trademarks of the publisher.

First published in Great Britain 2005
Harlequin Mills & Boon Limited,
Eton House, 18-24 Paradise Road, Richmond, Surrey TW9 1SR

© Dianne Despain 2005

ISBN 0 263 18850 7

Leabharlann Co. Mhuigheo
Mayo County Library

Set in Times Roman 10½ on 13¼ pt.
15-1205-52570

Printed and bound in Great Britain
by Antony Rowe Ltd, Chippenham, Wiltshire

CHAPTER ONE

"Your *hôpital* is all you have on your mind, *mon ami*. You should take the night off. Enjoy with me. Drink the champagne, look at the pretty women. All work and no play makes Dr Paul Killian a very old man very fast. And once you wither up and blow away, what will become of your *hôpital* then?" Bertrand Léandre threw back his head and laughed heartily, then took a puff of his big fat Cuban cigar. A mountain of a man in his tuxedo, he was big, broad and obviously the domineering factor in the room, domineering in every physical aspect. And the people at the party responded positively to him, hovering around him, listening and laughing.

All except Paul Killian, who was already tired. For them, it was a party. For him, it was work. He couldn't even remember when he'd taken the time to enjoy, and it was a pity because as parties went, Bertrand Léandre always threw the best. But raising funds for his hospital was a vital part of Paul's job now, and Bertrand had the funds Paul needed. More than that, he attracted the funds, so there was no turning his back on generosity, especially when he wanted to add a new children's wing and buy another whirlpool therapy tub.

Paul laughed. "All work and no play adds a whirlpool to

physical therapy." He tugged at the tight collar of his starched, white shirt. Tuxedos weren't his style. Neither were the silk bow-ties nor the stiff, shiny black shoes that protocol demanded with the formal ensemble. Horrible dress for a man who had gotten use to the garb of Kijé and found it not only fetching but comfortable. Gauzy pants, loose cotton shirts, sandals. If anybody had told him two years ago when he arrived on Kijé that the tops of his toes would soon be tanned, he would have laughed.

But they were now, as were the toes of every other fair-skinned person who spent their time in a tropical paradise. And that's what Kijé was. A tropical Caribbean paradise. Blue skies, blue waters and those legendary balmy breezes, none of which required formal garment.

But an evening in a tuxedo was part of the job, and shedding comfort for formality was worth all the bother because people, overall, were generous at these affairs. And he counted on that generosity to improve the condition of his hospital. Bottom line. That's what he was about. Finding the funds that made Killian Hospital run.

Paul flagged a passing waiter for a flute of ginger ale, because he bypassed the Dom Perignon at these affairs when he was representing the hospital and so much was at stake. "And as for the pretty women, even if I did notice them, when would I have the time, Bertrand? You know my life. Do you think a woman in her right mind would even look twice at me if she knew that I was destined to run off at a moment's notice?" He'd been married to a beautiful woman who hadn't been able to abide the lifestyle. She'd wanted to wake up every morning looking at his face on the pillow next to hers, which had turned out to be a rare occurrence in their marriage.

Traditional domesticity wasn't his strong suit, but it's what Joanna had needed. Too bad they hadn't known that before they'd married. "Tried it once, *mon ami*, and you know how that turned out." And trying it twice wasn't on his agenda. So he didn't tempt himself. All work and no play…the substance of Dr Paul Killian.

Bertrand snorted. "You are too hard on yourself. Even the most untraditional of marriages can be the most wonderful, if the two people involved are meant to be together. You and the other Dr Killian were not meant to be together no matter what the circumstances. In marriage, *mon ami*, that's what you get: either meant to be or meant *not* to be. You, unfortunately, fell into the *not* category, and it had nothing to do with your absences." He smiled wistfully, then sighed. "I know these things, Paul."

Bertrand referred to his own marriage to the late Dr Gabriella Léandre. She had been a pioneer in heart surgery, living most of her life in Paris while her husband had lived in Miami and Kijé. It had worked nicely for them, but it hadn't worked at all for Paul and Joanna, and he was fully aware that many, maybe even most, of the shortfalls in that fiasco of a marriage had been his. "You were the fortunate one in your marriage, but for me, like you said, it wasn't meant to be. So now I have my work and it makes me happy." He cast Bertrand a well-rehearsed smile, one he used so often in affairs such as this. "And speaking of work, I need to get back to it."

Paul took a sip of his ginger ale, glancing around to size up the guests there this evening. Most of them he knew, some he did not. Some would be generous donors, others would refer him to their accountant for that obligatory contribution— the one that would make Bertrand Léandre take notice of them—and still others would simply decline. But that's the way it was in his world, and he didn't take it personally. "So tell me, Bertrand, to whom should I be talking instead of you now? Who will be the best use of my time here tonight?"

"My, but you have become proficient, haven't you?"

"I've had a good teacher," Paul responded, his eyes still scanning the crowd.

"Always the work, Paul." Bertrand tsk-tsked him, shaking his head. "Always the work, and yet you are so rarely there to see the work. All that education and you reduce yourself to a common beggar." He shook his head again, this time frowning. "It's such a waste, my friend. You could be the head of a great hospital somewhere. You have the talents and I have connections. Would you like for me to see what I can do for you?"

Paul smiled patiently. They'd had this discussion before. Many times before. "About picking some pockets for me, yes, please see what you can do. But about finding me another job, you know the answer. I have my job." And he loved it. Passionately. Because in the end, people who couldn't afford treatment from other sources received treatment at his hospital. At no cost. So maybe he didn't doctor in the traditional sense so much now, but the outcome was the same. People who needed help were helped.

Paul glanced away from Bertrand to the entryway, to the woman standing there, looking around the room. His breath caught in his throat for an instant. Then he blinked. Had she stumbled into the wrong party? Dressed in khaki shorts, a blue T-shirt and hiking boots and standing there so elegantly in her jungle attire amid all the sequins and silks and Ferragamo shoes, that had to be the case.

Whatever the reason, the Fates had sent her here only for him, and the man who *never* looked was already grateful for the gift, because she was the most stunning woman he'd ever seen in his life. With flawless skin and wild black hair hanging well past her shoulders, she was tall and lithe, and her legs... Dear God, those legs... Covering them in the formal wear all the other women at Bertrand's affair wore would have been a high crime.

Quite simply, everything about her took his breath away for in that moment as she stood there surveying the room and he surveyed her, it was just the two of them. Dim lights, soft jazz, and no one else. And as her eyes searched all the people and finally came to rest on his, he didn't hear the next words from Bertrand, neither did he hear any of the stifled gasps coming from the crowd over her audacity to gatecrash the affair dressed as she was.

No, he heard none of that because as her eyes finally met his, he heard only the pounding of his heart.

Then as she started to move across the room, her strides purposeful and not at all in the graceful manner he might have expected from one so exquisite, he found himself still drawn to her every movement—the way she pushed her hair back from her face, the way her shoulders swayed with each step she took, the way she moved through all glitz yet emerged as the most captivating person in the room.

No, he couldn't take his eyes off her. Didn't even try. Perhaps she was looking for directions to her rightful destination—a place to which he already ached to follow her.

But she didn't stop, not even when one of waiters approached her to offer champagne. She merely refused him with a gentle smile and continued on, showing to everyone who looked on that in a room full of tuxedos and designer gowns, that she was the standout, the one all eyes followed, and not because of her attire.

The farther into the room she moved, the more hushed it became, and by the time she reached the spot where Paul and Bertrand were standing, it was so quiet throughout, even the clinking of the champagne flutes on the waiters' trays seemed an intrusion.

Stopping there, she glanced up briefly at Bertrand Léandre, offering him a faint smile. "Papa," she said, pausing briefly as he bent to kiss her cheek. Then to Paul, "You are Dr Paul Killian, are you not?"

Paul nodded, and before he could utter a word she grabbed hold of his hand and started to pull him away from her father. "Good. My name is Dr Solange Léandre, and I must speak with you, Dr Killian. *Privately.*"

"You don't look like your photograph," Solange commented once they were in the hall. Then she smiled shyly, quickly adding, "I mean that in a good way. You look much better than your photo." He *was* much more handsome in person. Larger, too. Well over six feet tall, with light brown, slightly long and unkempt hair, blue eyes, perfect smile—yes, he was handsome, but in a way she'd certainly never considered worth a second look. Until now.

Dr Mauricio Raúl Muñoz had certainly been a handsome one. The type who'd *never* failed to turn her head and, in retrospect, the type she should have turned her head away from. He was shorter than Paul, with dark, wavy black hair, and those dark, brooding eyes. Solange shivered, and not in a good way, thinking about him. Mauricio had been, oh, so wrong for her. Three years wrong, as it turned out. "I saw your photo in the newspaper. You were posing with my father at one of his charity events, and he was donating some lab equipment to your hospital, I believe." Actually, she knew. She'd kept the copy and memorized Paul's face in the expectation of this meeting.

And, admittedly, she'd liked his smile in that photo. The same smile he was flashing at her right now. The one that was causing her to shiver again, but in a good way this time.

"I'm flattered that you remember me and, more than that, recognize me from the photo, because it wasn't very flattering." He chuckled. "It's true what they say about cameras. They put on ten pounds and, in my case, ten years."

Solange tossed him an impertinent smile. "Are you fishing for a compliment, Doctor?"

"Having you notice me was the best compliment you could have paid me." He snagged a flute of champagne from the tray of a waiter scurrying into the Salon Rose and handed it to Solange. "In my dreary life, that's a rare occurrence," he continued, grimacing. "Sadly, more rare these past two years than I should be admitting to a lady such as yourself. It makes me seem rather pathetic."

"I think we all get noticed where we want to be noticed, Doctor. Where and how." She took a sip of her champagne, then set the flute on a replica Queen Anne hall table against the wall behind her. "If you live a dreary life, I suspect that's by choice."

"Or necessity."

"I understand necessity. That's the reason I'm here. Out of necessity." She drew in a deep breath. That sounded a bit too sharp-edged, she thought. But she was nervous, and this was so important. "Forgive me for getting straight to the point." To take the edge off, she retrieved the champagne and drank it all in one effort. She simply tilted the glass back and let the bubbly slide down her throat in the hope that it would brace her for this, as well as make her a little more mellow.

"Basically, what I want is a place to send my patients for various tests. Yours is a private hospital, your money pays for the tests, your equipment performs them, and I thought that proper protocol demanded me asking you before I started sending people your way. A medical courtesy."

"Your patients?" he questioned.

"Rurals, Doctor. I work up in the Massif des Montagnes Noires, traveling to the various villages."

"And the rurals rarely seek out traditional medicine, Doctor?" Paul asked. "In my two years here on Kijé, I can recall only one or two instances where they came to the hospital. Most of the time they don't trust us."

Solange smiled. "It's a challenge. I understand that. But for me, I like knowing there's help available if I need it. Someplace to send my patients if the situation warrants it."

"And how are you going to persuade them to come to me?"

"I have a partner who travels with me who is the persuasive one. I think I'll leave getting them here up to him."

"Another doctor?"

Solange shook her head. "A monk. He's wandered the mountains of Kijé for thirty years, getting to know the rurals, and they trust him."

"You can only mean Frère Léon, the one-man medical mission. I haven't seen him for a while and I was wondering where he was." He chuckled. "He is always a bit of a crusader, isn't he, trying to set up better medical facilities throughout the island?"

"And I'm the conquest of one of his recent crusades." Solange laughed. "So now I travel about half my time, and I do have a little infirmary operating at an old mission halfway up the mountain. We offer basic care there, but not X-rays and lab work. And that's what I want from you, Doctor. The ancillary services. Something that will give me the diagnostic tools I need."

Paul chuckled. "And here I was hoping that you'd sought me out for something other than my *ancillary* services."

"Sorry to disappoint you, but yours is the closest facility to my mountain, and I've heard you do brilliant work there."

"Ah, you do know how to crush a man, Doctor."

"Not crush, Doctor. Persuade." She laughed. "So is it working? Are you persuaded yet? Or do I have more work to do here?"

"Tell me who you are, Dr Léandre. You said you're a doctor, and it's obvious you're Bertrand's daughter. Actually, I'm surprised he's never mentioned having a family, other than…Gabriella."

"My mother," Solange whispered. Gone ten years now, mention of her mother still brought a lump to her throat. "My father doesn't get past my mother, so I'm not surprised you haven't heard of me from him. But to answer your question, I'm a doctor, specializing in public health and infectious disease. I've was working in a Miami clinic that closed up just over a year ago." Locked up tight, building on the auction block, and a fiancé who'd thought it had been time to go upscale with their joint medical practice. Except, silly her, the legalities on the contract had made it *his* medical practice, *his* building, *his* decision. "So I came here to Kijé, took to the mountains, and the rest, as they say, is history." Solange glanced over Paul's shoulder to the door of Salon Rose, where her father's party had already resumed with the next round of champagne and caviar, and where her father loomed, scowling in the doorway, a single malt Scotch in one hand and a cigar in the other. "Do you have a room here at the hotel, Dr Killian? Someplace where we can talk privately, without my father's scrutiny? He thinks I make bad career decisions and his position on this would be to install me as a medical director in a large hospital somewhere. His solution is always the biggest and the best."

Paul chuckled. "I've had that offer myself. Just a few minutes ago, actually."

"Then he must like you. Which is high praise, as my father is an exacting man who keeps most people at arm's length." She smiled at her father, who acknowledged it with a half-hearted attempt at a smile. "He really hates being left out of this, you know."

"Am I detecting a little angst in your family situation?"

"A little. My sister, Solaina, was always better with Papa. I was better with Maman, I think. Her way to love her family was to nurture it. His way was to control it." She shrugged. "But I didn't come here to tell you my family history, Doctor." *Here, at* L'Hôtel de Brise d'Océan. How ironic, after all these years. As a child, she'd played on the white sandy beaches outside, dined in the world-class dining room, slept in the down-filled beds. And she'd loved that life. But that had been so long ago, in more innocent times when she had been young. Now she wasn't affected by the trappings. They were nice, as were the memories, but the aspiration to be part of that life again was so far removed from her reality she had a hard time even imagining it.

Mauricio had aspired to the trappings, though. Wife, children, a nice home far, far away from the way they started out helping the needy. All desires he'd sneaked in on her, a little at a time. "So can we go somewhere and talk for a while? You tell me what you have to offer and I'll tell you how I'd like to make use of it."

"Do you know how long it's been since anybody said something like that to me?" Paul said, chuckling. "Like I said before, you really do know how to crush a man."

He grinned at her, and the warmth in his smile almost distracted her. But she had to be careful. *The Mission, Sol*. "Look. I want to apologize for the way I stormed in there…" She glanced down at her attire, then over at his. "I don't always think these things through before I act, and when I read in the Port Georges paper that my father was to be here this evening, *with you*, I suppose you can see that I didn't think it through as far as I should have. So why don't you go back in there, enjoy the rest of the party, and maybe later we could meet for a chat, figure out how your hospital can work for my patients. If certain days are better than others for routine tests, what specific kinds of tests you're set up to do…"

"And I don't suppose I could convince you to join me?"

She laughed. "Not a chance. I've had my share of that life and, trust me, I don't belong in there. So you go back, and when you've finished, I'll be waiting in the lobby for you."

"You don't give up, do you?" he asked.

"We all do what we have to do, don't we? Especially if we believe in it." She wasn't getting a good read of him yet. Definitely not a *no*, but also not a *yes*. He had kind eyes, though—eyes she caught herself trusting easily.

"Would you be more comfortable in the bar than my hotel

room, or maybe having dinner?" He glanced at her father. "The lobster here is fabulous."

"This is not a date, Dr Killian," Solange countered, not sure what to make of this whole thing. It was promising, but on what level? Personal, professional? Was he simply scouting a bedmate for the night or honestly interested in listening to her? "I don't need to be entertained in a bar, and I certainly don't need lobster, fabulous or otherwise."

Paul chuckled. "You really *don't* give up."

"I really *can't* give up. My medical practice is expanding now that the villagers in the mountains are getting used to me, and even trusting me. And I want to get this arrangement taken care of before there's an urgent need. I'm assuming that you'll make your facilities available to my patients. Or am I mistaken?"

"Of course I'll make my facilities available."

"Which leaves us to the ways, Dr Killian."

"And the means, Dr Léandre. I always have to figure in the means." Paul glanced over at her father, who was beginning to inch closer to hear the conversation. "So about that lobster dinner…?"

Solange smiled. In spite of her caution, she liked him. He was to the point, but charmingly so. And he did so tempt her to veer off course for a little while. "I do like lobster, but I'm not dressed for the dining room and I'm sure there's a dress code, so I'm afraid I'll have to pass on the offer." Safe comeback, and on the personal side, all she wanted was safe.

Paul took Solange's arm. "You're dressed better than anyone you'll find in the dining room, in my opinion anyway. But I'm afraid you're right about a dress code, so—"

Solange thrust her palm out to stop him. "So this is where you get me up to your room?"

"Purely lobster. And talk. I can give you an hour, but that's all."

He was back to business. That was good, because that's all she could cope with. "So I'll take that hour, *and* your lobster."

He arched his eyebrows suggestively. "More's the pity this is only business, because you're good, Dr Léandre." Paul laughed as he held out his arm to escort her to his hotel room. "*Very good.*"

"So are you, Dr Killian." Good, she was sure, in ways she would never know.

CHAPTER TWO

PAUL's room was heaven. Solange followed him through the door and simply stopped and stared before she was all the way inside. Pure heaven, just the way she remembered these rooms to be from her childhood. Red tile floor, two colonial king-sized beds, a vast picture window with a marvelous view of the pristine beach outside, and of the blue ocean beyond it.

Even though it was nearly dark outside now, in the pinks and golds of the twilight she could see a sailboat making its way slowly to port, its tall white sails fluttering lazily in the early evening breeze. She'd gone sailing out there with her family so many times. Her parents, her sister Solaina. Those had been good times, and she almost ached from the memory of them. But that had been so long ago, and nothing now, or in her future, was about sailboats or any of the other luxuries with which she'd grown up. She didn't miss them much, though, because she had the memories, and nothing now could come close to that.

"The bathroom," Solange whispered, crossing over to take a peek at the bathtub. White porcelain, deep, and curved in a way she was sure would fit to her well. Solange sighed wistfully. Only a few months up in the mountains and she'd already forgotten how nice a long soak in the tub could feel. Now it was a matter of a quick, usually cold, shower. Function over luxury. And time necessitated expediency because, no matter where she was, she was expected someplace else.

But this bathroom was so nice, she did indulge herself the fantasy of it all for a moment, picking up the scallop-sculpted soap nestled into a large abalone shell sitting at the washbasin. The lavender scent of it wafted up to greet her, and she quickly replaced the soap in its abalone shell for fear that getting caught up in the luxuries here would distract her.

"Feel free to use it," Paul said. "Any of it. All of it."

She laughed. "Am I being that obvious?"

"Like a kid in a candy store."

"Out in the jungle there aren't any such luxuries. We have buildings and we have the basics, but lavender soap... Frère Léon buys lye soap from one of the villages and, believe me, it doesn't come close to smelling this nice." On her way out of the bathroom, Solange stepped in front of the mirror over the vanity, almost afraid to take a look.

Her first glance at herself was such a shock. "*Mon Dieu!*" she whispered. Slowly lifting her hand to her face, she brushed it across her cheek, then her lips, then she raised it to her hair and ran her fingers through it. "I've aged so much," she said. Her eyes were almost hollow, her hair so wild. And she was so thin... Turning away, she smiled self-consciously. "I haven't been in front of a mirror for months and after all this time I'm afraid it's quite a shock."

"Then we must be looking at two different images, because what I'm seeing is absolutely stunning."

"Kind words, Doctor, but not the ones I want to hear from you."

"That's right. You came to discuss lab tests and X-rays." He laughed. "It seems to be a family trait. Your father's a stubborn man—"

"I'm not stubborn," Solange interrupted, turning out the bathroom light and stepping out into the hallway. "I wouldn't argue the point over my father being stubborn, but I like to consider myself persistent." She smiled at him, hoping not to seem too pushy. "Persistent with a purpose."

"And I always thought that was called stubborn. My mistake." Paul placed the palm of his right hand flat against his chest and gave her a slight bow. "And my sincerest apologies to the *persistent* lady. I'll never make that mistake again."

"Accepted," she said, laughing. Paul was quite the charmer, and she shouldn't be paying attention to him in a personal sense, or even liking him as anything other than a business contact. But she did, and it was very foolish! She knew that. She'd had a charmer for three years and look how that had turned out.

So why was she still susceptible? Especially when anything personal had the potential to make this situation between Paul and her difficult. She needed professional—colleague to colleague. Nothing else. Maybe not ever again, because it was turning out that being on her own wasn't as bad as she'd feared it might have been. In fact, she rather liked her life, coming and going as she pleased. Nothing but the work to dictate her time and attention. Without Mauricio, life was good now, better than it had been in a long time, and she aimed to keep it that way. *Meaning no more charmers!*

"So now that you stand corrected about my *persistence*, shall we work out the details of your hospital schedule and arrange the best way for my patients to be seen there?"

Solange went to sit on one of the two rattan chairs in a grouping at the end of the beds.

"That's direct," he said. "And just when I thought I might get lucky."

"Lucky, as in…?" She tossed him an exaggerated puzzled look.

"Apparently as in it's just my luck to be in a hotel room with the most beautiful woman on the island and all she wants to do is schedule X-rays."

"I think you're finally catching on," Solange teased.

"Believe me, I may have caught on, but I don't have to like it."

"Is this how you raise your funds? Flirt with the women until they open up their…" Solange tossed him a sly wink "…purses to you?"

"If you had a purse, would *that* technique work on you?"

"Flirting? Not a chance. I learned how to be impervious to that technique, as you call it, a long time ago."

"Sounds bad."

"At the time, yes, it was bad. In a look back, it was the best thing that could have happened to me."

Paul seated himself across from Solange, and plucked an orange from the fruit basket on the table between them. "Me, too," he commented casually, breaking it apart and handing her a section. "Difficult at the time, and in a much broader perspective, it was the best thing that could have happened to *her*."

"Her?" Solange asked before she popped the orange into her mouth.

He grinned. "She got everything she wanted—the husband at her side, lots of children. The life she wanted that I couldn't give her."

After swallowing her orange, Solange asked, "And what did you get?"

"The life I wanted. I travel and I'm not too tied into the domestic scene at this stage of my life, which is a good thing. I can't be the *perfect* husband, or any kind of a good husband for that matter, and continue to do what I do. Couldn't then either, so we split and everybody's happy."

"You still have contact with her?"

Paul nodded. "Our parting was, as they say, amicable. No hard feelings and we do talk every few months. Mostly because she wants to know what's going on at the hospital, though. But it's not strained. And you?"

"Hard feelings. *Really* hard feelings." No need to say more. This conversation was becoming much too personal. But Paul was so easy to talk to, and listen to, and she was going to have to keep up her guard to avoid getting caught up in every little shade. Or in him.

"Let me guess. No one has captured your heart since."

"I haven't dated since," Solange said, matter-of-factly. "One of my neighbors in Miami gave it a try...chocolates and champagne."

"And?"

She wrinkled her nose, recalling the memory. "And he had all that champagne and chocolate to himself." Plus a pile of clothes tossed onto the sidewalk. One of her moodier moments, admittedly. But such a good one!

Paul handed Solange another section of orange and practically drooled, watching her eat it. Attraction aside, and he was surely attracted to her, this was crazy. Pure craziness. He had work to do, and in another few days he'd be back in the States. And here he was...so distracted he didn't want to go back to Bertrand's party at all, back to all the wealth.

That was something he *never* allowed.

Even so, with one hundred prospective donors awaiting his return to Salon Rose, here he was sitting in a rattan chair, sharing a piece of fruit with her like he had all the time in the world. All because he wanted to spend more time with an entanglement he'd promised himself he wouldn't go after again. Or at least not for a very long time. *And just look at him now!*

Paul shook the tension out of his shoulders, handed Solange the last section of the orange, and tossed the peels at the trash can across the room. He missed, and they landed on the floor. But he didn't go to get them. Couldn't go. Couldn't walk away from Solange. Not now. "My lab technician Bijou will be able to give you a better idea of how she's able to schedule patients for lab procedures. The same is true for Zac, my X-ray tech. Unless we have an emergency, they maintain their own schedules and workloads, and they're both much better equipped to tell you the best way to handle your patients. Also, they'll be able to give you a better idea of what will be available to you."

"Then I can't wait to meet Bijou and Zac." Solange popped the last section of orange into her mouth, leaning back in the chair to chew it—slowly, deliberately. Seductively. At least, *he* was seduced. Never before had he considered the way a person chewed to be sexy, but he was so transfixed watching Solange that when she stopped he wondered how long he'd been staring.

He cleared his throat, and leaned back in his own chair. "Tell me about your little infirmary." Not that he needed to know. But his transaction with Solange had essentially ended now. She would talk to his technicians about making future arrangements for any patients she might want to send to his hospital and, for all intents and purposes, he was out of the mix. If he left the room this instant, it wouldn't matter. She had his consent, and that's all she'd come there for. Proper protocol, as she called it.

He wasn't ready to end it, though. Not yet.

"It's a nice little facility," she said. "Frère Léon and some of the men of his order set it up in the hope that one of their own might be able to run it. But none of their own are medically trained, and apparently it sat empty for well over a year before they approached me. And to be honest, I expanded their idea a bit. Talked them into letting me spend most of my time on house calls, which works out nicely."

"So, I've been on Kijé two years now, and I know a little something about the people here. Based on what I've seen, are the rurals accepting you as a doctor?"

"That's the hard part. They're accepting of my medicine, but wary of me...being a woman. I've made friends, and have several people who do trust me. But many don't. Of course, I've only been on the mountain three months now. It all takes time."

"And who minds the infirmary while you're out in the rural areas?"

"I have two nurses. But don't confuse my definition of infirmary with yours because we have one examination room and beds for four patients. That's all, and in the three months I've been on Kijé, I've had exactly six patients spend the night. Which is why I don't spend much time there."

"But you're supplied?"

"Quite nicely, actually. My father helps me out and Frère Léon is certainly a wonderful provider. We have running water and electricity from a generator at The Mission and well-stocked medical supplies... We're doing quite well. Better now, since you have what I don't."

"Have you ever thought about extending the services at your infirmary? Adding that lab equipment or an X-ray machine?"

"I do think about it all the time. But the simple fact is, we're too remote up there in the mountains. And for the numbers of people who would even consent to any kind of testing we might do, it's a waste of money. I can do the simple things like the PPD or blood sugar with what I have." Common tests for tuberculosis and diabetes. "But I can't do a CBC." Complete blood count. "Of course, I might have only one or two patients a month who would require a CBC, so even if our location would accommodate the necessary equipment, the patient load would not."

"Which is where I come in."

Solange nodded. "You and your hospital. Oh, and that lobster dinner you promised me—is that still part of the deal?"

Dinner was a simple affair. Lobster, an array of fresh, sautéed vegetables, baked potatoes, freshly made crusty bread. And, oh, yes, ice cream for dessert. With a wonderful dessert selection, Solange chose plain vanilla ice cream, and Paul couldn't talk her into the truffle or the tiramisu or even the *crème brûlée*. It had to be the vanilla ice cream. "You have a hearty appetite," Paul commented.

She laughed. "One thing I've learned, living with only the barest of necessities, is that when you do manage the good fortune to have something extra, you never, ever waste it. Especially lobster." She longingly eyed a chunk of succulent tail meat sitting on his plate. "You're not going to let that go to waste, are you?"

"With you around, apparently not." He speared it with the seafood fork, dragged it through the butter and held it out for her. As her fingers brushed his in taking the fork, a shiver ran up his spine and he caught himself wondering what it would be like to feed her that lobster with his fingers.

His fingers? Where the hell had that come from? Paul shook his head, trying to rid himself of that image. He really didn't know enough about her to be having these feelings. No, he didn't know nearly enough to be so blithering. "So tell me about your clinic in Miami," he said, trying to get his mind off the obvious.

"I was there three years. It was closing so I left."

Matter-of-fact words. Too matter-of-fact for the flash of anger he saw in her eyes. "Did you like the work?" he asked, trying to return to neutral ground.

"I loved the work," she snapped. "But that wasn't enough."

No, definitely not neutral ground. And to top it all off, her body language was going rigid. What had been friendly and open was suddenly cold and defensive, which meant he was wandering down the wrong path with this topic. Or probably any topic right now, judging from the scowl onto her face. "Sorry, I didn't mean to pry."

"I'm sorry about being so abrupt. It's an old wound that, apparently, isn't as well healed as I thought it was."

Old wound. At least it wasn't something he'd said, and he was glad about that.

"He hurt you badly, didn't he?" Paul refilled her wineglass and handed it to her. He might have liked to have made a night of it here, sitting and talking, but the truth was, he did have to get back to Bertrand's party shortly. The night was still quite young, and he had work to do. Funny, that! In a way, he was like Solange—going only so far, then pulling away with an excuse of work. It was safe. He knew it. Apparently, she knew it, too.

"He pulled the rug out from under me. I thought we were partners in more ways than one, but we weren't, as it happened. So I suppose you could say that I needed the rug pulled out. After three years, when you haven't made the right commitments, they aren't going to come along. Not in the sense that you want them to, anyway."

"You mean as in marriage?"

"It went far beyond that. We were medical partners." She paused, shaking her head vehemently. "Let me rephrase that. I *thought* we were medical partners, but in the end I was his employee, with no say in the practice. He decided it was time to go upscale, sold out and moved on up."

"And here you are."

"Here I am, doing what I want to be doing. Simple, predictable story. I let him do it, he did it. But the ending was as it should have been."

"Even though you're not over him."

"I'm completely over him. Maybe a little bitter around the edges about the circumstances of my medical practice with him, and definitely much wiser when it comes to life and matters of the heart. I should have taken a better look at him from the start."

"There are a lot of things you don't see when you fall in love. Either it sneaks up on you or blindsides you and, however it happens, it's not exactly an objective period in your life, is it? What you're looking at isn't necessarily what's really there."

"But you got over it, didn't you?" Solange asked him, bending forward to spoon up a bite of the ice cream.

"Better than I thought I would once I saw that Joanna wasn't the one for me, and I certainly wasn't the one for her. She got happy when she left me, and the hell of it is, looking back, I'm not sure I ever saw her truly happy with me."

"Did you get happy, too, when it was over?"

"Oddly enough, yes. Even though I didn't end up with the love of my life like she did, I got happy. Maybe it's because I wasn't so torn between my obligations any longer—obligations like trying keeping the hospital funded and keeping my wife happy at the same time, which was nearly impossible since the expectations of both seemed to always be on a collision course with each other. So, you said you're a little bitter, but is there any happiness in there for you now that you're single again?"

"I'm getting happy. I've got a ways to go, but the biggest part, I think, is that I've found what I was meant to do. My work defines me, and being back here on Kijé, traipsing around in the mountains with Frère Léon, that's what makes me happy."

Paul spooned a bite of ice cream from the bowl, then raised it in the air for a toast. "Here's to getting happy, one and all."

Solange chinked ice-cream spoons with him, then smiled shyly. "I really am sorry for getting so grumpy and making all kinds of assumptions. Mood swings... Living in the mountains will do that to you, I think."

"Apology accepted. Look, I've got to get back to Bertrand's little soirée. Believe me, I'd much rather spend the rest of the evening here with you, but that's what I do. I mingle with the people who will give me money, and there's a lot of money to be had in there if I make the right connections. So what I'd like to do is take you back to my hospital in the morning, introduce you to the staff, get you acquainted with what we have available, then maybe travel up the mountain with you, if that's OK. I have a few days before I need to leave Kijé, and since I'm going to get to show you mine, I'd love to have you show me yours."

"You *are* talking hospital?" she asked, scooping up the last bite of ice cream.

"Unfortunately, yes."

"And just why would you want to come back to my infirmary?"

"I need a reason?"

Solange laughed, then wrinkled her nose at him. "You're not an easy man, Dr Killian."

"That's the reason," he replied. "The way you do that cute little wrinkle to your nose. I'd like to spend more time with that wrinkle, get to know it better."

"Not good enough since that wrinkle is strictly off limits to everybody now."

"OK, I'd like to catch up with Frère Léon. Haven't seen him for quite a while and he's an old friend, so I'd like to see how he's doing. Give him his yearly physical."

"His physical? You're telling me you're Frère Léon's physician?"

Paul dropped his linen napkin onto the table, then stood. "Yep, that's what I'm telling you. So, have you made sleeping arrangements for the night?"

"The hotel is booked solid. I checked earlier. So I thought I'd probably go sleep in my truck."

"Stay here tonight, Solange. In my room. I have two beds, and I know you're dying to stretch out in the bathtub."

"I appreciate the offer, Paul, but I'll be fine in the truck. Really."

He knew she would. Solange had a survivor's heart. "Then you take the room *alone* tonight and *I'll* sleep in the truck. And you can help yourself to all the bubble bath and perfumed soap you want."

"I don't want to chase you out of your bed. Believe me, I've spent many nights in the truck. It's not a problem."

"Where did you do your medical residency?"

"Chicago. Cook County Hospital."

Cook County—one of the oldest and largest charity hospitals in the United States. That was impressive because by reputation it was demanding and by patient load grueling.

"Well, as you were at Cook County, I'm sure that you're familiar with the old medical tradition called the on-call room?" Where beleaguered doctors on call, needed to be up and working at a moment's notice, piled together in rooms full of beds simply to grab a little sleep any way they could, anywhere they could, until their services were next required.

"I've had my share of familiarity in on-call rooms. Hated the snorers, though." She wrinkled her nose again. "Had enough of sleeping next to those in my days."

"I don't snore," he said, heading to the door. "So consider this your on-call room for the night. Take either of the beds you want, and if *you* snore, and it disturbs me, I'll wake you up and send you out to your truck. OK?"

Asking her to sleep in his room? Inviting her back to his hospital? Even thinking into next week and next month and next year and seeing Solange there? Outside in the hall, Paul leaned against the wall and shut his eyes. This was crazy. Absolutely crazy! "Not smart," he muttered, straightening up and tugging his silk bow tie back into place.

Even now, though, realizing just how stupid this was, simply thinking about Solange Léandre still took his breath away.

In the bathtub, Solange watched the steam mist over the mirror before she shut her eyes and allowed herself to drift. Maybe eating Paul's lobster, stretching out in his bubble bath and sleeping in his bed weren't the wisest things to do... Maybe they were downright stupid... But Paul wasn't like Mauricio, even though she tried to force the similarities on him. Not like him at all, which was the best thing that had happened to her in a long while. And he was so attractive, something she really shouldn't be thinking about, even though she was. He was nice, too. A man who knew what he was about, and she liked that.

On that pleasant note Solange relaxed into her bath, let the raspberry-scented bubbles slide over her skin, and wiped everything out of her mind. Everything except, perhaps, the notion of what it might feel like to have Paul immersed in the raspberry bubbles with her.

CHAPTER THREE

SOLANGE was fascinated by the little town of Abbeville. She hadn't been there before, and as she drove through the streets, following Paul's SUV, she was tempted to stop and get out, walk around, greet the people, soak in the atmosphere. It was a friendly place from first impressions. Friendly, and alive with color. The short, straight dirt roads were lined with tiny wood-frame houses, each one painted in hues so bright it looked like an artist's palette gone wild. Pinks and blues, reds and oranges...no color was too bold. No yard so ornamented and cluttered as to be gaudy either, judging from the cement statuary submitting to every imaginable form—elves and geese and pigs—all adorning the grassy patches outside the houses. And there were old rusty vehicles parked where the statuary wasn't sitting, and over-stuffed couches and indoor beds pulled out onto the porches for easy outdoor living and to catch the cool, evening Kijé breezes.

It was an amazing splash of culture. Noisy street vendors selling everything from their push carts—fruits, shoes, cigarettes. People waving to her as she drove by, children chasing balls and kicking cans across the dirt road, dogs stretched out napping in the middle of the road and too lazy to move out of the way as Paul honked at them.

Seeing Abbeville in its fullest, everyday array made her love Kijé all the more.

"How did you find this place?" she asked Paul several minutes later, as they approached the wood-framed Killian Hospital. Unlike the other structures in Abbeville, it was white. Plain, dignified white, with no cement statuary, furniture or old vehicles in its yard.

"Frère Léon."

"He does get around, doesn't he?"

Paul nodded, laughing. "When Joanna and I arrived to work with one of the humanitarian organizations here, he approached us with the idea of starting it. There was no medical care anywhere near here, which made it the perfect place, not just in terms of proximity to so many of the smaller towns in this region but because the people here are outstanding—friendly, helpful. I think this is where I first realized that paradise isn't about a beach chair, an unsullied stretch of sand and a tropical drink with a paper umbrella and a skewer full of fruit. And I owe it all to Frère Léon, a man of great insight...*and* foresight, who stranded me here for a day. He simply dumped me in the street and drove away in..." he glanced back at her truck "...that!"

"You, too?" Solange laughed. "He took me up to the old mission church in the mountains and didn't come back for two days. By the time he returned to fetch me, I had two nurses and a short line of patients waiting to be seen. And I didn't leave."

"Tricky devil," Paul said, taking Solange by the arm and leading her up to the entrance of the hospital.

He was all that, and more. Frère Léon had been her port in a very rough storm, and she owed him everything. "I don't know what I would do without him." She was pleased Paul shared her affection for the monk. In a way, it made them seem much closer already.

"We think there's a possibility we might have a case of Pott's disease," Dr Allain Sebastian stated, his nose buried in a medical chart. Allain was second in command of Killian Hospital, after Isabella Mordecai, who was the chief of staff there. Paul had made the decision to leave the medical workings of the hospital in their capable hands when it had turned out that he had been spending more and more time away. It had been a good decision, too, because they were a dynamic team. Hardworking, smart and, best of all, dedicated to the kind of care the hospital stood for.

"Allain's from an infectious disease program out of Boston," he explained to Solange, as they both donned masks before entering the area of the patient wards. It was protocol. Universal precautions, no matter what the situation. Better safe and inconvenienced in some instances than sorry. "When he heard about all the perks we offer here, he couldn't wait to apply for a job."

"Perks!" Allain snorted, fighting back a grin. "Long hours, no pay. And the accommodations… I gave up a townhouse with a Jacuzzi for a room with a sink." He winked at Solange. "What more could a man want?" He extended his hand to her. "I've been on my feet sixteen hours already and I've barely begun."

"Believe me, I know those hours." Solange laughed. "My name is Solange Léandre. *Dr* Solange Léandre. And, no, I'm not here to work."

"That's too bad, because I was already looking forward to

eight straight hours of uninterrupted sleep tonight. Haven't had one of those in months. So, are you open to bribes, Solange? Anything I own just to have you cover one shift for me."

Solange smiled first at Allain, then at Paul. "I'm usually open to bribes, especially lavender soap and lobster dinners, but since I've had my share of those recently, I'm afraid I wouldn't be awfully susceptible right now."

"Lavender soap and lobster dinner?" Allain raised a skeptical eyebrow at Paul. "Don't think I'll ask."

"Don't think I'd tell even if you did," she replied, smiling shyly at him. She could feel the heat rising in her cheeks over the ideas Allain was forming, ideas she'd had herself.

"Well, I do have a fondness for lobster, if you should ever have any left over. Don't care much for the lavender scent, though. At least, not on me. So, Solange, is this a social call or a professional one?" Pudgy and short, with a ruddy complexion and red hair, Allain Sebastian stepped back and appraised both Solange and Paul. Then he gave them a big, toothy grin.

"She's here to demand one more hour a day from you," Paul teased, faking a frown.

"Stop that!" Solange laughed, hitting playfully at Paul. "It should only take half an hour of Allain's time. You'll have the good doctor thinking I'm quite the mercenary."

"And just when I finally quit believing all those rumors about the pirates on the Caribbean seas," Allain quipped.

"It's not quite a pirate's ransom that I want," Solange explained. "Just a few routine tests for my patients whenever the need arises. I have a little medical infirmary up in the mountains, and I don't have the facilities for X-rays and lab work. I came to make arrangements here."

Actually, Frère Léon had insisted she make the arrangements and had practically shoved her off the side of the mountain to get her to do it. Now she was here, she was glad she'd come. This was a wonderful facility. Neat, tidy. Clean. Paul was terrific. Allain was, too. And it was nice getting herself back into the medical community, around doctors, after being away from it this past year. Even if this was just a cordial acquaintance since she would rarely, if ever, have the need to come here again in person, she was enjoying the camaraderie. The working dynamics here were good, and the chumminess fun. Nothing like her last months at her clinic in Miami.

"Well, for your patients, Solange, I always have an extra half-hour. But in the meantime, I need to get back to that possible case of Pott's because, to me, it's just not quacking like Pott's."

"Quacking?" Solange asked.

"Quacking," Allain repeated. "You know the old saying, 'If it looks like a duck, and it quacks like a duck…'"

"Then it must be a duck," Solange supplied. "And your Pott's disease isn't quacking like Pott's disease." Pott's disease, a form of tuberculosis, occurred when the TB bacillus escaped the lung and traveled throughout the body and lodged in the spine. It was a common occurrence, and in the Caribbean the leading cause of paralysis in young men.

"Something like that. He has the right symptoms, especially the paralysis below the waist. But he's latent." Latent TB, meaning he tested positive for exposure to the disease but didn't have the actual disease. "And I couldn't find any significant case history of Pott's in latent TB."

"Well, you're right about that. You don't normally see Pott's in latent," Solange replied. Then she deferred to Paul. "Sorry. I shouldn't be stepping in here. I'm just the visitor."

"The visitor who's welcome to step in any place, any time she wishes," Paul said, gesturing for Allain and Solange to follow him to the small, two-bed room where the patient, Agwe Bourg, was snoozing quietly in bed. "We don't really have any kind of a medical hierarchy here so, by all means, step in, comment, offer opinion, order tests. It's all welcome."

"Why do I get the feeling that I'm working?" Solange asked, laughing.

"Because Paul's like that. He just sneaks it in on you. And watch your pockets, Doctor. He's been known to pick a few of those on occasion."

"You left out the part where I make you think it was *your* idea to have your pockets picked," Paul added, opening the door and walking straight to the bedside of Agwe Bourg, a man, probably in his mid-thirties, who had a wife and seven children depending on this diagnosis. "So in spite of Mr Bourg's being latent, why would you suspect Pott's, Dr Sebastian?" Paul asked, keeping his voice low so not to disturb his patient.

"Like I said, he has the latent diagnosis, which puts him close to the disease. Maybe not right on it, but definitely close. And he does have the other symptoms—paralysis, general malaise." He drew in a deep breath, then let it out slowly through his mask. "But it's not Pott's. At least, that's my gut instinct."

Paul nodded, but said nothing, so Allain continued. "He's in the right age category, though, so that's not a rule-out." Often, diseases that were difficult to diagnose were given a final diagnosis by ruling out other conditions and symptoms. Rule out enough factors, then take a good hard look at what was left.

Paul nodded again, looking down at Agwe Bourg. "Fever?"

"Yes," Allain said.

"Weight loss?"

Allain nodded. "He says he has no appetite, and we haven't been able to get him to eat a thing."

"Cold abscess?" Solange asked, pulling up a chair to sit next to Agwe. An abscess, cold to the touch, was almost always present in Pott's.

"No. I've checked him twice, and so far he's negative for a cold abscess. That doesn't mean it won't develop, but Mr Bourg has been ill for a couple of weeks now, according to his wife, so it's not likely to appear at this point."

"That's good," Solange said, taking hold of Agwe Bourg's hand. "Standing over a patient, looking down at him, is so impersonal. I like being on their level. It makes for a better rapport." Gently, she gave the man's hand a squeeze, then watched as he squeezed back. "Good muscle tone. Good reflexes. Do either of you have a stethoscope?"

Paul pulled one from his pocket and handed it to her. She listened to Agwe's breath sounds for a moment, then handed the stethoscope back. "Clear lungs." She looked at Agwe. "Do you have a cough?"

He shrugged to indicate he didn't understand. So Solange repeated the question in Creole—the language spoken by most of the rurals. On Kijé, the languages were a mixed bag. Broken English, Creole, and, among the uppercrust, French.

"OK, no," Agwe said.

"Do you think the TB might be going active?" Allain asked, totally captivated by Solange's gentle bedside manner.

Paul noticed that the younger doctor had barely taken a breath as he watched Solange check Mr Bourg. It was such a subtle lesson she was teaching. One about eliminating the impersonal tone in medical practice and making the patient feel cared for. A chair at the side of the bed, a squeeze of the hand...these were such simple little things that mattered so much. With all the haste and hurry around his hospital, Paul thought about how often the simple things were overlooked, and he admired Solange for remembering. Somehow, she would always manage them no matter how rushed she was, and he admired that even more.

"His TB going active is a possibility," Solange said. "It can do that, depending upon certain factors—more exposure to the active disease, other physical illnesses or weaknesses. But I think Mr Bourg is doing fine. Probably suffering from some kind of secondary infection outside Pott's, if I'm not mistaken. Because when I took his hand, he shifted in the bed and moved his legs. Just a little, mind you, but I saw movement." Her eyes crinkled a smile at Paul over the top of her mask. "You did, too, didn't you?"

Paul nodded, his eyes smiling back. "So I think we're all in agreement now that's it's probably not Pott's disease, and Mr Bourg is one lucky man because of it. But we'll still need some blood tests to rule it out."

Solaina bent forward to speak to Agwe, to which he responded by pulling down his mask and giving her a great big grin, revealing a mouth full of rotten brown teeth. Friendly, but infected. And there it was. An uncomplicated thing now. "There, Doctors, is the source of our initial infection, I believe. Our patient here said he's been pulling out his own teeth."

Paul looked down at Solange over the top of his mask, and the instant their eyes met, the look they shared confirmed a diagnosis for Agwe Bourg. "Osteomyelitis," they said at the same time.

"Told you it wasn't quacking like a duck," Allain chimed in. "And if it's osteomyelitis, the pain's probably so bad that Mr Bourg just quit moving to avoid it. So I guess he yanked his infected tooth and the infection spread."

"When you don't have a dentist, that's what you do. And, personally, I've always hated the dentist," Solange commented, shuddering. "But pulling your own teeth... I think I'd rather cut myself open and remove my own appendix, *without anesthesia*, over pulling out my teeth."

"Well, I'm pretty good at removing an appendix, if you ever have a need," Allain said, already bending over Agwe with a penlight and peering into his mouth. "And from the looks of things in here, I'd guess I'm about to get good with dental extractions, because we've got at least three potential sources for infection festering away right now." Dental infections were often the cause of serious, even fatal, illnesses that resulted from harmful bacteria escaping into the bloodstream. When they lodged in the heart, which was common, it was called bacterial endocarditis, and out here, more often than not, it was fatal. And when they lodged in the bone, it was called osteomyelitis, and could be fatal if not treated, but if caught it was treatable. Today was Agwe Bourg's lucky day. He was treatable.

"Allain's the enthusiastic kind," Paul commented. "He'll take on anything."

"Especially eight straight hours of sleep," Allain called after them as Paul and Solange left the tiny room. "If anybody's interested in giving them to me."

"He's a good doctor," Paul said once Allain was out of earshot. "Young, a little unorthodox, enthusiastic, and great instincts. I'm glad Frère Léon found him."

"Another one?"

Paul nodded. "Like I said, he's a tricky devil."

Solange laid her hand on Paul's arm and gave him a gentle squeeze. "With or without Frère Léon, this is a nice hospital, Paul. If I weren't already involved up in the mountains, I'd be honored to work here."

"And I would be honored to have you work here." He glanced down at her hand on his arm, and drew in a sharp breath. Another one of the simple things Solange did, and he could feel the sparks of it all the way down to his toes.

"We're divided into several large wards, accommodating sixteen beds maximum in each one. Plus, as you're noticing, we've got patients in the halls." Bed after bed lining the walls. "With any luck, we'll be starting a building project in a few months to add on two more patient wards and a children's ward."

Times like this, when he needed so much more, gave Paul the overwhelming urge to get back out there and find the support. "Right now we're over the maximum capacity, and we're beginning to feel it because, like the rest of the medical world, we're short-staffed."

"Did you anticipate this kind of need when you set up here?"

"I anticipated a few patients straggling in every day, and I'll be the first one to admit that I was wrong." He shook his head. "It's frustrating at times, but we don't turn anybody away." Paul stepped aside to allow Solange her first good look into one of the men's wards. "It's not modern by any standards, but it works quite nicely," he explained.

"Modern?" Solange exclaimed, stepping up to look

through the glass in the door. "This is wonderful, Paul. Even my clinic in Miami wasn't this nice." Of course, Mauricio had cut corners every time he'd found one to cut, saving that money for his upscale move. *Their upscale move.* Only she hadn't known it at the time. "And, believe me, if I could ever come anywhere close to something like this, I'd think I'd died and gone to heaven."

It was a bare-essentials set-up. A bed, a bedside stand, a patient—sixteen of them lined up in two well-kept rows of eight each. There wasn't much room in the ward, but it was tidy. "Thanks to Frère Léon?" she asked.

"In part, yes. He supplied the craftsmen to get it built. Locals who wanted a hospital nearby. He had an army of them, and it went up much like an Amish barn-raising. The men working, the women feeding the men, the children playing around the area." He chuckled. "I think Frère Léon told them if they didn't get it done quickly, Joanna and I might change our minds and leave."

"The tricky devil," Solange laughed.

"And you said you're in an old mission chapel?"

Solange nodded. "Ayida and Keskeya—my nurses—and I actually live in the chapel, and the infirmary is in a brand-new building separate from it." It was a nice, comfortable set-up and she loved it. "The whole compound was a cloister a century ago, but the monks moved to the other side of the mountains about seventy years ago to be closer to the major throughways." She smiled, thinking about how glad she was they'd left the old compound behind. It was the perfect place, where several roads led in and out. The villagers were using them now to come to The Mission, as it was called, for clinic days, where medical services were offered at the infirmary instead of out in the villages. "How many people work here, at your hospital?" she asked.

"Right now I have three physicians, all specializing in infectious diseases, besides myself, although I don't really count myself as a physician. And I have twice that many nurses and nurse aides. We also have a lab technician and an X-ray technician. Like I said, we're short-staffed according to our patient load, but we make do." He smiled uncomfortably. "Of course, we're doing much better on staff than you are, aren't we?"

A young woman dressed in khaki shorts and a T-shirt scurried to the bedside of an older man to change an IV bag, and Solange watched the interchange between nurse and patient. Pleasant, efficient. Paul had a nice concern here. "Actually, we're quite satisfactory in numbers. I'm out a good bit of the time, and Ayida and Keskeya take care of the infirmary while I'm away. And if I need to be there as a doctor, I'm there. People don't get all fussy and bothered over schedules and appointments out where we are, so it works out splendidly for us."

Paul led Solange to a door marked "TB", and they stood outside, looking in through the window. "Do you treat a lot of TB?" she asked.

"About half our patient beds are devoted to it. Not enough to call us a TB hospital, but enough that we keep busy with it. The wards I'm going to add will be much larger than our normal wards, and they'll be specifically for people with TB. I'm actually going to build a separate building for it, so the patients won't have to be quite so confined.

"But the good thing about our TB program is that we actually have good luck with the treatment and cure rate when the patients get to us in time, then continue to take their medicines for that interminably long year after diagnosis. Which many of them do, now that they know there's help available. We try to dose them here in the mornings, if they'll come here... It's the easiest way to keep on top of things. And we do some education on TB symptoms, making it more likely that if people recognize the symptoms they'll come to us in the early stages rather than later on. Care to join me inside?"

Paul strolled through the doorway into the ward, with Solange following. "One of the biggest problems we have is that so many of the people quit once their treatment is started and they feel better. We get a lot of recurrences, and every single one of the men in this ward fall into that category. They took their INH, felt better, stopped it, and now they're back. Only most of them have some form of drug resistance going now, which is what usually happens when you stop treatment in mid-course. And the next time around TB is so much harder to treat.

"So to lessen our workload, we hunt our patients down when we can, just to make sure we don't get them back in here in another few months in the condition most of these men are in." He gestured to the men in the ward and most of them responded with a friendly wave.

"Sometimes the condition doesn't recur, though," Solange said. "Sometimes TB doesn't come back."

"Sometimes, but rarely. If we could keep them here the whole time..." He shrugged. "But you don't treat TB that way any more."

"Dr Paul!" a middle-aged woman shouted as she ran down the short hallway toward them. "She came in with the baby already on the way out. And it's not waiting to get born, except the cord's coming first."

"What?" Paul snapped, spinning around to Gigon Giroir, one of his trained nurses.

"The baby is not waiting, but the cord is beatin' it out. She's prolapsing, Doctor, and it's not looking good 'cos she's having some hard, fast contractions."

Paul and Solange exchanged knowing glances before they ran down the hall, following Gigon, who ran so fast she looked like a sprinter heading for the finish line. "Start an IV," Paul shouted after her. "Get set up for a Caesarean section and go find Dr Mordecai."

"Do you deliver babies often?" Solange called.

"No, they go to the village midwife if it's a normal delivery. We just get the bad ones."

Solange followed Paul into the small procedure room, where a very pregnant woman was moaning on the examination table. Gigon was already slipping an IV catheter into the mother-to-be, whispering soothing words…words that seemed to have some effect since the mother wasn't screaming at the top of her lungs.

A nursing aide cracked the valve of a green oxygen cylinder to blow off any settling dust, then hooked rubber tubing to it in preparation of placing a mask over the patient's face.

The initial hiss of the oxygen blast startled the patient, who struggled tried to sit up, but Solange stepped up to her side and laid a reassuring hand on her shoulder to keep her down while the aide fastened the mask over her face then scurried around the bed to pile pillows under the pregnant woman's bottom. That made it easier to keep the umbilicus from tangling around the baby's neck.

"Where's Isabella?" Paul called to Gigon. Dr Isabella Mordecai was an experienced surgeon who had chosen to practice infectious disease medicine over surgery. "I'd much rather she did the surgery than me."

"She's got someone down there on the active ward, spittin' up blood something awful," Gigon said. "She'll get here when she can. Dr Allain just got one of the patients ready to pull some teeth, and Dr Wally is in town, doing the follow-up on dosing this afternoon. So it's up to you." She glanced over at Solange. "Unless that one's a doctor who can do it."

Paul glanced over at Solange, too, as he wrapped a blood-pressure cuff around the expectant mother's arm and started to pump the rubber bulb. "So, can you do a C-section?" he asked her. "Not that I'd put you in the position of doing it if you didn't want to. But I'm not exactly a sterling example of a surgeon, and if you'd…" Instead of finishing, he stuck the stethoscope into his ears and inflated the blood-pressure cuff, then nodded seconds later as the hiss of deflating air showed the woman's blood pressure to be normal.

"I can do it," Solange said, tightening her mask. It had been a while since she'd done it in practice, but she'd had a whole year in which she'd studied up on procedures she might have gone a bit rusty on. C-sections were included in that. So she was ready. "Do you have some kind of anesthetic?"

"Just morphine, as the procedures we do are normally minor."

"That means I'll have to be fast, doesn't it?" she commented, pressing a stethoscope to the mother's belly to see if she could hear a fetal heartbeat. Wrong kind of stethoscope, though. All she could hear were the normal tummy gurgles, which sounded good, actually. "Because we can't risk having the morphine cross the blood barrier into the baby."

"Can you be fast?" he asked.

"If you can second me with the baby. Keep the cord free and make sure the baby's head doesn't come popping out. And deliver it, actually, when the time comes."

"Deliver it?"

Solange nodded. "Lift it out while I'm attending to the mother."

He shrugged. "Sure. I can deliver it."

"Good. Then I say let's get on with this C-section."

The woman on the table moaned with her latest contraction, and begged for help. "Please, Doctor," she cried.

"What's your name?" Solange asked.

"Brigitte," she strained to reply. "Brigitte Sonnier."

"Well, Brigitte, you have a baby wanting to get born, and I'm just about ready to get started." She stepped to the end of the bed to see how much of the cord had prolapsed. A good bit of it, she discovered. But not so much she thought the baby would get tangled.

"You make my baby OK?" Brigitte asked, her eyes full of fear.

Solange went back to the head of the bed and gave Brigitte's hand a squeeze. "Just relax. In another few minutes, you're going to be a mother."

Gigon gave her a nod, then pointed her in the direction of the scrub area. Paul followed her in. "You don't like to hold newborns?" he asked, as he ran his bare arms under the water.

No, she didn't hold newborns now, if she didn't have to. There were too much of a painful reminder... "I like to concentrate on one patient at a time. I'll take care of the mother, you take care of the baby. Two patients, two doctors."

Solange scrubbed, dried her arms on a sterile towel, slipped a plastic protective shield over her face, then snapped into her gloves. By the time she was gowned and back in the tiny surgery, Brigitte's contractions were harder and coming faster. The baby was starting to crown!

"Please," Brigitte begged. "Help my baby."

"Don't push," Solange told her. "Even if you feel the urge, *don't push*." Pulling on a second pair of gloves—an old, double-gloving procedure that had long ago become a habit—Solange took one last look at her patient. "You're going to be just fine," she whispered, as Gigon drew up the morphine solution to stick into the IV bag. "We're giving you something to help with the pain, and as soon as it has had time to start working we'll get that baby right out of you."

"Please, Doctor," the woman whispered, "don't let my baby die!"

"Relax," Solange whispered. "Take a deep breath for me, and close your eyes…"

Gigon pulled back the sheet and gown, and prepped Brigitte's swollen belly with antiseptic. This would be fast, Solange knew. As hard as the baby was trying to push out of there right now, this procedure couldn't be fast enough. "I'm good to go," she said. "Paul?"

"Keeping the cord clear, and ready when you are."

The procedure was swift and uneventful. At the same time Paul lifted the baby from her mother's womb, Gigon removed the bit of umbilicus that had wrapped itself around the baby's neck, and all was well. Brigitte Sonnier's daughter came into the world in perfect order, kicking and screaming and pretty well angry at everybody for the inconvenience.

Solange didn't look at that precious life Paul cupped in his hands as Gigon applied a couple of clamps to the cord and snipped between them. She kept her attention focused squarely on her patient until Isabella Mordecai ran into the room, tying a fresh mask around her face. "Sorry I couldn't get here sooner but Clarence Didier was having a bout with hemoptysis—" coughing up blood "—and I didn't want to leave him alone."

"How's he doing?" Paul asked, finally stepping back from the operating table.

"Fine now. It wasn't serious, but he was scared. Want me to close up for you?" she asked. "I'm all scrubbed up and ready to go. And I'm pretty good at stitches."

"I'd love for you to close up for me," Solange said, "because I'm terrible at stitches." Isabella was a big woman. Large frame, robust, long brown hair pulled back into a braid. If there was one word that could be used to describe Isabella Mordecai, it was jovial. Which was a trait in high demand. "Can't even sew on a button."

"Good thing our patient doesn't need a button, then. You go on and get out of here now. Everybody's in good hands."

Solange didn't doubt that for a minute, and everyone in the room heaved a collective sigh while Isabella put in the first stitch. After which Paul staggered to a chair out in the hallway and collapsed. "Damn," he gasped, shutting his eyes. "I can't believe I just did that."

"What? Deliver a baby?" Solange avoided the chair next to him and slid down the wall until she was sprawled out on the floor.

"Believe me, I'm much better at delivering money," he said, holding out two very shaky hands for Solange to see. "Too long past patient care and too long with the ledger, and this is what you get." He tucked his shaking hands up under his arms.

"But you did a brilliant job, Paul."

"I delivered a baby, Solange."

"Brilliantly." She laughed. "And the only one complaining was the baby. I'd say that makes for a smashing success."

"And I need an antacid, and some tranquilizers."

"You're too hard on yourself, I think. You were a very good doctor in there. Good instincts, good reactions."

"I haven't done any kind of significant patient care in years, Solange. And what I just did in there was more than significant. But that's just not the kind of doctor I am any more, and I'm glad you were here to do the hard part."

He sounded melancholy, she thought. Steady, but a bit sad? "Would you rather practice medicine than raise funds?" she asked, on a hunch.

"I've always wanted to practice medicine, and I expect that at some point in my career I'll get back to it. And there was a time I thought myself good at it. But when I get into a situation like what just happened, I realize how much I don't belong in there any longer. Even in two years I've become very out of practice."

"Raising money is important, though. What you do makes it possible for someone like Brigitte to have her baby delivered safely. That baby would have died, you know, if the hospital wasn't here."

"Well, what I do may be just as important, but not nearly so noble, is it?" He stood, then smiled down at her. A sad smile, she thought. Certainly one that gave her an honest look into his heart. He was a noble man, even if he didn't recognize it. A very noble man, and she admired him for that.

"I'll be ready to leave with you in about an hour," he said, as he walked away. "Got a little paperwork to take care of, then I'll be good to go."

Paul did an amazing thing at this hospital. She could see it everywhere...an amazing, and a *very* needed, thing. Perhaps it was selfish of her to think this, but she was so glad he'd been the one to stay here when his marriage had broken up. Somehow, she couldn't imagine this little hospital thriving under anyone but Paul.

Professional opinion, of course. Strictly professional.

CHAPTER FOUR

THE first half-hour on the way to the mountain was bumpy and slow, with the emphasis on slow. Pitted, rutted dirt roads took over from the smooth dirt roads leading from Abbeville, and the farther from Abbeville Solange and Paul drove into the rural reaches, the more pitted and rutted those dirt roads became. In kilometers, the drive was fairly short, but in endurance it was a long-distance marathon, and the winner was the one who, instead of arriving at the finish line first, arrived there without sore muscles and a bruised backside.

"I think you're just too soft, spending so much time in padded office chairs and airplane seats." Solange laughed, swerving to avoid yet another pothole. They'd pulled in behind a *tap-tap* twenty minutes before, which she'd refused to pass, even though the exhaust fumes from Kijé's infamous public transportation heaved from the old bus in a cloud of dense smoke, making a mad dash straight into the front seat of her truck. Of course, rolling down the windows to get some fresh air wasn't a problem, because there were no windows in her truck. No windshield either.

"Trust me," Paul said, switching positions in the front seat next to her for the thirtieth time in thirty minutes, "I've been in some cushioned office chairs bumpier than this. At least in the figurative sense. And sometimes the figurative bruises hurt a lot more than the literal ones, especially when you've poured out your heart and soul in the hope of a donation and all you get is a scowl."

"We had a hard time getting funds into our clinic in Miami. A couple of the hospitals helped us, and we had some neighborhood organizations. But we operated on a very thin line, not always sure if we could even pay the light bill. It was a good practice, though. In spite of the hardships, it was satisfying because in the end people who had nowhere else to turn were getting help."

"And you loved that, didn't you?"

"Totally. That's what medicine should be about, you know? At least, my version of it. But you're the same way, aren't you? Always looking out for the humanitarian obligations."

"I am now, but in the beginning, when I came here with Joanna, it was more about appeasing her until she got over the notion, which I truly believed she would in a month or two. And me…well, I was counting the days until I could get myself into a Monday-through-Friday, nine-to-five position, taking on-call once a week and golfing every Saturday morning."

"So let me guess. You found yourself here on Kijé. And you found your cause, something that you wanted more than a condo and a Mercedes in your garage."

"Two," he corrected. "In my vision, there were always two of them in the garage. And you're correct about discovering myself here. After about a month I realized that I loved the work and the cause. I was needed here in a way I would never be needed in a cushy practice anywhere else, and that need became *my* need, because, as much as they needed me, I needed them even more. The root of being a good doctor, I think. Talk about a turnaround. You plan a life around one thing then find out it's not the life you want."

"Mauricio," Solange murmured. "My turnaround. Three years with him then he made a mad dash for all the things *you* thought you wanted and found out you didn't." Of course, the timing had had everything to do with his decision. He might have stayed around a while longer, but in the end the result would have been the same. Mauricio would have gone because she couldn't fulfill his entire dream. When she'd left, she'd only beaten him to it.

"Three years. Ouch. That's a big bite out of a life."

"It really is," she agreed. "But it wasn't bad. Not all of it. And I truly think that being with Mauricio was where I found myself. Otherwise, if my father had gotten his way, I might have ended up across the hall from you in the cushy practice. It happened to my sister, going along with my father in a sense, and she's had some amazing administrative jobs."

"She's a doctor?"

"Doctor of nursing."

"And she succumbed to Bertrand's indomitable will?"

"He's been a big force in our lives. He has a strong sense of what's right for everybody around him, and he doesn't back down from it too easily. *As you probably know.* But for Solaina, he was a huge force behind the kinds of jobs she has taken. At least, until she met her husband; traded in administrative budgets for everyday bedpans and became ecstatic about her new life. Naturally, Papa isn't too happy about it." A melancholy smiled touched Solange's lips, disappearing almost instantly. "I'm the rebellious one, though. I've always leaned toward doing just the opposite of what he wanted right from the start, and one of the things he wanted most was to have me in a respectable medical practice. So, if I'd given in, who knows...?"

"You went the public health route to spite him?"

"No. I went the public health route *in spite of him* because I fell in love with it while I was doing my residency. It has been the bane of my father's existence ever since." She laughed. "But he sends care packages to the mission—drugs, supplies, medical journal classified ads of major job openings around the world. I think he's a humanitarian at heart, something he got from my mother. But his way of acting like a humanitarian is a little overbearing. It's part of that whole vision of his...what's right, what's wrong."

"And Bertrand Léandre's way is always right."

"No matter what," Solange added. "My mother tempered him, though. She was amazing about that. And I think the way he is now is more of a reaction to not having her with him any more. She was the part that completed him."

"I would have liked your mother," Paul said gently.

"You would have loved my mother," Solange whispered reverently. She didn't cry now about her mother, but thinking about her still brought a lump to her throat. Everything Solange was, she credited to her mother, and she only wished she might have the chance someday to be the kind of mother *her* mother had been.

Paul opened his mouth to respond, then choked on a puff of smoke from the *tap-tap*. "Maybe we could pull over and let it go on ahead?" he sputtered, trying to fan the fumes away with his hands.

"And deprive ourselves of an awesome familiarity of an island icon?" She laughed as she slowed down to back away from the exhaust fumes.

"Love the icon, hate its souvenir." He took in a deep breath, then coughed again.

"I've got some masks in the glove box," she said. "Never leave home without them."

"I'm fine," he replied, wiping his eyes. "The *tap-tap* only got one of my lungs, and I'm not permanently blinded from the smoke."

"City boy," she teased, slowing down even more.

A *tap-tap* was a bus usually, or sometimes a truck, used for public transportation. The way to spot a *tap-tap* was by its decoration—every color of the rainbow painted into every design known to artists around the world. The one they were following was red, orange, yellow, green and purple-striped, with large red apples in a border around the top and larger white swans floating on blue ponds spaced in sporadic locations over the striping. Replicas of the red and yellow Kijé flag, surrounded by gold-painted fringe, waved majestically over the swans.

This tap-tap was full of noisy people, and at least a dozen adult men sat on the top of it, waving at the people they passed. They'd waved at Paul and Solange off and on now for forty minutes in traditional Kijé manner—raising the hand and wiggling the fingers. "I've always loved the *tap-tap*," Solange said, her voice almost wistful. "When I was a little girl I always wanted to ride in one. All those pretty colors and decorations…what little girl wouldn't want to?"

"Let me guess. Your father wouldn't allow you to."

"I never asked him because I was afraid he would say no, then I'd have go behind his back and take a ride. So instead I used to sneak out and ride whenever I could. It was always such a great adventure.

"Oh, we'll be turning off the main highway pretty soon, and after that you may *wish* you were on a road where a *tap-tap* could get through ahead of you."

"That bad?" Paul returned another friendly wave to toothy, grinning man on top of the *tap-tap* who was being rather persistent about eliciting a wave from him.

"I wouldn't call it bad so much as adventurous, like my *tap-tap* rides." He was so good-natured about this, she thought. Running off into places unknown with a virtual stranger. She liked his company, whatever his real reason for coming.

"You're not allergic to donkeys, are you?"

Paul twisted around in his seat and cast her a dubious glance. "I don't think I'm even going to ask what that's about," he said. "I've always believed that some things are better left unsaid, especially when they have anything to do with me and a donkey."

The trip behind the *tap-tap* lasted another half hour until finally Solange turned off the road onto something that didn't even resemble a road. They were definitely well on the way into the jungle. This wasn't a road used by many, Paul noted, and he was forced to set his jaw to keep it from jarring so hard his teeth would break. "I don't suppose the donkey's saddle is padded, is it?" he asked.

"City boy," Solange teased.

"Does it show that much?"

"Only a city boy would ask that question!" She laughed, pointing down at his feet. "And only a city boy would wear nice white shoes where we're going."

He glanced down, wincing. Brand-new. "So what you're telling me here is that—"

"City boy," she broke in. "That's all I'm saying. You're a city boy, and it shows."

"You say that as if it's a bad thing."

"Out here, it can be. Especially in white shoes." She shook her head skeptically. "You'll stand out, Paul. They'll see you coming and I'm afraid there's nothing I'll be able to do to help you." She bit back a smile, keeping her eyes straight ahead on the road.

He could see the taunting turn of her lips. Lips he would much rather kiss than watch. *That* was a dangerous notion, one he needed to put right out of his head. "Why is it that I've never heard about your infirmary?" he asked, trying to get his mind off what he was seeing. And feeling.

She gave him a quick, sideways glance, arching her eyebrows in faint surprise. "I think that part of the reason is because we're in the mountains. We're isolated. The villagers are farmers and craftsmen, and their way of life is somewhere between modern and old-fashioned. Some of the people live in huts with thatched banana-frond roofs, some in houses much like you see in Abbeville, and there are no facilities to speak of—no convenient little grocery stores, no apothecaries, no stores to buy yard goods, not even any street vendors like in Abbeville. Put it all together, and the whole region is easy to overlook."

Solange swerved off the road onto one that was even worse. "And sometimes it's easier to not see, because seeing brings responsibility." She pointed to a clump of houses off to the side of the road where barefooted children were lugging gourds and buckets full of water back from the stream. "That's

Ambrose," she said. "We'll be stopping there for a few minutes while I make a house call and organize our next mode of transportation."

It was a nice clean little settlement, all lined up along a central road, with weathered wood-frame houses evenly spaced along both sides. The road wasn't paved. The houses weren't painted like in Abbeville, and there weren't sidewalks or yard statuary. But Ambrose looked friendly, Paul decided as they drove along the one and only road that divided a field of sugar cane in two. A thin man in a straw hat stepped up to the side of the road, waving the traditional Kijé wave at them. "Maman Solange," he called, cheerfully. "We been waiting for you to come back."

"They call you mother?" Paul asked.

Solange nodded. "Everybody needs one sometimes, I suppose. And it's an honor, because it means they trust me. Look, I'll just be a few minutes. I've got to see a man about his *écrouelles*."

Paul noticed Solange looking back at him, smiling coyly. Probably because it was that obvious he had no idea what she was talking about. *Écrouelles?*

"Want to come with me, Paul?" she asked, her face a canvas of innocent enticement—head tilted down, playfully widened eyes looking up at him, just the hint of a smile touching her lips.

Solange *was* playing with him now. She was good at it, and he was, oh, so willing. But did it show? he wondered. "And just what would you expect from me if I did go with you to your rendezvous with *écrouelles*?"

"Maybe offer a second opinion?"

"Only a *second* opinion?"

"Perhaps a first opinion, if that's what you like. The order of these things really doesn't matter. You first, me first. How about I let you choose who goes first?" She brushed a few strands of straying hair from her face, nodding toward her destination. "Are you coming?"

"Only if you tell me, first, what *écrouelles* is. Animal, vegetable, or mineral? A nice pastry? One of those would be awfully good just about now. Something with a custard filling, perhaps?"

"I'm not sure about the custard, but I can guarantee that you'll find scrofula."

Scrofula—a tubercular infection of the skin of the neck, most often caused by inhaling air contaminated with the organisms causing tuberculosis. After the bacteria spread through the body the result was normally a rubbery enlargement of the lymph nodes, in the neck most commonly. Every once in a while, a case presented at the hospital, but in rural areas like this, scrofula was more common. "You just ruined quite the fantasy for me, you know. I could almost taste the custard." And almost see her licking it from her fingers…one finger at a time, slowly, seductively. Paul blinked hard, twice, to rid himself of the images seeping in.

Solange laughed. "Don't think I can find any custard for you, but would goat's milk do?" She pointed at a nanny goat wandering down the street, the bell dangling from a collar around her neck jingling away with each and every step.

"Just not the same. Custard…goat's milk." He cringed, shaking his head. "So I guess you'll have to tell me about the scrofula."

"In the locals I probably see two cases a month," Solange said. "Never very serious, but a persistent problem." She reached over the bed of the truck and grabbed her backpack. "So, since you're not going to find a pastry at the end of your quest today, how about a piece of candy? In fact, I know several children here in Ambrose who would love some candy. And playing candyman is infinitely more fun than dealing with scrofula." Opening the pack, she continued, "Every time they filled up the complimentary mints bowl at the hotel I emptied it. I managed to get quite a bit."

On inspection, Paul discovered that Solange's backpack was filled to overflowing with candy and fruit. Why wasn't he surprised she'd done that? More than that, why hadn't he thought of that himself? "I'm not going to find a boiled lobster in here somewhere, am I?" he asked, scooping out a handful of candy and stuffing it in his pocket.

"They also change the fruit every day and what's left over is tossed out. One of the maids let me have the discards."

"I think you could beat me at my own begging game with very little effort," Paul said, chuckling. He, for one, could turn down nothing for which she asked. Money, candy...his heart.

His heart? Where had that come from? Because he sure wasn't going to go that far, even though he was beginning to see just how easy that could be.

"Your game and mine, Paul, are the same game, I think. We merely play it differently. Oh, and don't let the children take advantage of you. Give them their piece of candy, and if you have a soft heart maybe a second piece. The adults might like a treat, too, especially some of the older people. And in one of my packs you'll find a bunch of grapes. Grandmère Prejean sits in a rocking chair on her porch most days. She has arthritis, so she never goes anywhere. Her house is the last on the left." She pointed down the road. "Give her a few pieces of candy, too."

Solange turned and walked into the house nearest them, her medical bag swinging back and forth at her side. Paul watched until she disappeared into the dark interior before he set off on his candy run, still thinking about the previous night when he and Solange had eaten lobster. An amazing night. And one he shouldn't be extending in any sense. His track record in relationships aside, he simply didn't have the time. Quite honestly, he didn't have the energy either. Everything he had was for the hospital, and there were no leftovers. Not even for Solange. Not that she would have him even if he did have the time and energy. He was just going to have to keep reminding himself of the vital facts and quit fantasizing himself into something more. That's all there was to it.

By the time he came to the last house, where he expected to find Grandmère Prejean, Paul had given away an ample supply of candy. "Is she here?" he asked a scraggly old dog curled up in the rocking chair where the old lady should have been sitting.

The dog opened its left eye to take a look at Paul, then shut it again. Probably too lazy and fat to get up and approach a total stranger, Paul decided as he looked at the flock of chickens pecking around in the dirt beneath the porch. There was a goat standing near the gateway, watching him with the same marked disinterest as the dog. But no Grandmère Prejean. "So, where is she?" he called out to the black and white mongrel, hoping Grandmère Prejean might overhear, as he stepped through the gate, sidestepped his way by the goat and shuffled through the chickens to get to the porch. "Is she home?"

The dog bared its teeth, more out of habit than the need to be territorial, but it didn't attempt to stand up, maintaining its roost on the worn old wicker rocker as Paul walked past it. "Hello," he called into the house. *"Bonjour, Grandmère Prejean!"* Her house was typical of those he'd seen in most of the rural villages. Small, plain, efficient, the elemental style of well-weathered boards capped by banana fronds. "Grandmère Prejean? Are you here?"

Paul listened for a response. "I have something from Maman Solange for you," he called when no one inside answered. Cautiously, he inched back the curtains hanging over the doorway and braved a peek inside.

The little house was alight with candles. All sizes, all shapes. Votive candles and pillars. Tapers and many, many Santaria candles. It was an amazing, flickering fantasyland, and he was drawn instantly to the shadowy images dancing round the room, simple, everyday images in the dark that the fire glow made magical. "Grandmère Prejean," he ventured again, as he stepped in.

Several seconds passed before his eyes to adjusted to the odd illuminations pirouetting about him, and because he was wary of stumbling around, risking breaking something he couldn't yet discern, he stayed put at the door. "Are you here?" he whispered. "Maman Solange sent me here with some grapes for you." He spoke in English because he didn't speak the other languages used in Kijé, even though it was doubtful she would understand anything of what he said other than Solange's name.

"Maldyok!" Grandmère Prejean screamed from the corner of the room in which she was hunched. *"Maldyok!"* she screeched again, clinging to her spot and not advancing on him.

His heart jumped to his throat. *Heart in his throat...* he'd read that phrase all his life, and now he knew what it felt like;

a huge lump he couldn't swallow. At least, not right away. Of course, it was a muscular contraction. He reasoned that immediately, but it still didn't reason away the fact that his heart rate had doubled. "Maman Solange," he said, extending the grapes in front of him for her to see. "From Maman Solange." He could see her now. A diminutive woman, probably not even five feet tall, she was gripping an old wooden cane in her tiny hand, shaking it at him, ready to defend herself with it. Fierce little lady. And she'd scared him to death. He was glad Solange hadn't been there to see it.

"I'm sorry," he said, holding up his free hand as if she were pointing a gun at him rather than a stick. Paul took a step back into the door curtain, straight into the matted, black and white dog that had finally decided it was time to wander in and do a little something more than merely bare his teeth and growl. The dog made a half-hearted lunge for him, in slow motion, and Paul was glad it was an old dog, because the mutt's apparent arthritis was the only thing that gave him enough time to move out of the way. Two steps to the side, and the dog stopped to contemplate this new dilemma.

"*Partir ici!*" Grandmère Prejean screamed, still shaking her cane. Get out! "*Maldyok!*"

"Better *maldyok* than *pedisyon*. *Maldyok* is only the evil eye. Meaning she believes you're casting the evil eye on her for some horrible reason. Most likely you're envious of her because she is one of the wealthiest women in the village. But the good news is that *maldyok* is easy to cure. You simply remove the source of the evil eye." Solange laughed, grabbing the grapes from Paul's hand. As she crossed the room, she scratched the confused dog on the head and held out the stem of grapes for Grandmère Prejean. "But if she'd been screaming *pedisyon*, then you'd be in big trouble, city boy, because that's an illness in which a woman thinks she's pregnant, and *pedisyon* arrests that pregnancy, meaning it's put into some sort of hibernation, even for years, until a cure is obtained and the pregnancy can resume. *Pedisyon* has a long-lasting effect. And eventually it could come with the obligation of fatherhood." She tucked a few pieces of candy into the old woman's apron, then gave her a big hug.

After a few minutes of conversation between the women, Grandmère Prejean was apparently convinced that Paul meant her no harm, because she surrendered her cane to the corner next to the fireplace, took a seat at a small table in the kitchen area and plucked her first grape off the stem. "She's still not convinced about you," Solange told Paul as she took his arm and led him out the door. "But she trusts me, even though she did warn me to be very careful of you."

"Warn you against me?" He chuckled. "And just what does she imagine I'll do to you?"

Solange shooed her way through the clump of nettled chickens, then tossed a bruised apple to the goat. "Sometimes it's difficult to find a literal translation between the languages, but I think the translation of this is close to something like witched. She thinks you'll witch me. Or bewitch me."

"I think it's the other way around. You're the one witching me." Paul headed for the truck, but Solange pulled him back and dragged him in the opposite direction from where she'd parked it. Then she pointed to three donkeys. One had his duffle bag and Solange's backpacks tied to it. The other two looked suspiciously like their transportation for the next leg of the journey. Bare-backed transportation at that!

"No, she was pretty clear about it." Solange spun around

and looked him straight in the eyes, then smiled. "Blue is an unusual eye color around here. All of us dark-eyed people do tend to become nervous around them, and she told me that your eyes are going to witch me." She laughed. "And she also told me you're too jumpy."

"Not jumpy. Cautious." He stared back into her dark eyes. They were the most beautiful eyes he'd ever seen in his life. One step closer meant commitment and all the troubles that came with it. One step back meant safety, but for the life of him he couldn't take it. So he held his ground and forced himself to smile, instead of pulling her into his arms as he wanted to do. Doing this, his options were still open. "Are you nervous around blue eyes, as Grandmère Prejean is?"

"My mother had blue eyes, so I'm used to them," she said, trying to sound matter-of-fact, even though Paul's blue eyes were definitely making her nervous, as well as witching her.

CHAPTER FIVE

"I THOUGHT you said something about a padded saddle," Paul moaned after five minutes into their hour-long journey on the backs of two very gentle donkeys.

"Saddle? I believe it was your assumption that the saddle would be included in the travel package." Solange laughed, glancing up at the sky. It was turning overcast now. Up in the mountains the storms weren't as severe as they were nearer the coast, but the winds... "You get two choices—bareback or straw mat, and, believe me, the straw mat, with all those little sharp ends sticking out, is a torture device in itself. You're better off with only your gauze separating you from Gertie. Gertie's happier that way, too, and, trust me, you want to keep her happy."

He winced as the donkey took a sharp turn to avoid a tree stump in the path and nearly bumped him off her back. "I don't suppose she understands the concept of light-stepping, does she?" He righted himself and took a firmer grip on the rein.

"Gertie is as easy as they come. She, and the other two, Pete and Lulu, have been with me as long as I've been here. They were given to me by—"

"Let me guess. Frère Léon."

"Actually, one of the other monks. At Frère Léon's behest." She smiled. "The tricky devil. He really does have influence, doesn't he?"

"Where he wants it. So, how did you meet him? I know you said he approached you to set up the infirmary and stranded you at the mission, but how did you meet him the first time?"

"He and my mother were... " Her voice trailed off. She was getting much too involved here. Personal chat was fine, but not every single detail of her life. Too much meant involvement, and she was fast learning that Paul would be very easy to have that involvement with. Too many reasons not to, though. Too many reasons on too many levels, and she'd already learned, *the hard way*, not to open herself up to anything that swerved her off course. It simply wasn't worth the risk.

Paul wasn't worth the risk. Especially now that her life was finally back on track.

"Look, city boy, it narrows down the farther we go along. But don't worry. If Gertie throws you, she knows the way home, so all you have to do is get yourself back up and follow her."

"Follow the donkey. All I can say is that this is the hardest house call I've ever made." Paul shifted positions to bring himself upright on Gertie's back.

"Somehow I don't picture you making house calls," she teased.

"Up until an hour ago, I didn't picture myself on the back of a donkey in pursuit of anything. But never say never, right?"

"Well, if it's any consolation, up until an hour ago Gertie didn't picture herself with you on her back." He was *definitely* good-natured, she thought, glancing up at the sky again, wondering how good-natured he'd be in the rain, because it was getting darker and they weren't going to beat the storm. The best they could do would be a stop-over. If they were lucky.

"I was married. Remember? Compared to that, Gertie is easy."

"So what happened to your marriage? You both loved the work, and I'd think that would have been such a strong bond between you." She shouldn't be prying. *She knew that.* Especially now that there was a picture of Paul with another woman planted firmly in her mind. It was silly, but she almost felt a little twinge of jealousy. "You don't have to answer that," she added hastily. "I shouldn't be butting into your private affairs."

"What went wrong wasn't exactly a secret, and Joanna and I weren't always quiet about it. Ask anyone at the hospital. In a way they even became part of the drama, taking bets on how long the marriage would last. If Gigon had allowed me into it I would have lost, because Joanna and I hung in there a lot longer than even we thought we would. But it's difficult moving on, isn't it? You've done that yourself."

"It is difficult," Solange agreed. "You try to convince yourself that it's something that it's not. Then you find a safe place in that lie and you're afraid to step outside it."

"But you never married him? Did he want to?"

"It was always something we put away for future discussions, and I'm not even sure which one of us put it away."

"Did you have an ugly parting? Or am I being too personal here?"

Solange spun around on Pete's back and looked at him. "You're being awfully personal but, yes, it was an ugly parting. Actually, the part leading up to it was ugly." More so than she cared to remember. Or reveal. "The parting itself was a relief. You know, like an upset stomach. It keeps getting worse and worse. All the churning, the nausea, and the pressure is building up, finally to the point that you feel like you're going to explode, then when you... Well, you know the rest of it." She wrinkled her nose in disgust. "And once you rid yourself of the whole messy episode, you feel so much better. It was unpleasant, but it was a relief. And you?"

Paul gave her an over-exaggerated, counterfeit cringe. "Nothing quite as ugly as all that. Actually, with Joanna and me, there was nothing much of anything. We just walked away quite civilly...no churning, nausea and definitely nothing exploding. And that was it."

"So you're the avowed bachelor now?" Solange asked, trying not to sound too interested, even though she was.

"Not so much avowed as practical. I have my life, and it's not going to change significantly in the near future, and it's not going to work out with someone who expects that it will change. And I don't mean to sound selfish or conceited about it, but it's my life and that's the choice I've made for it."

Those were words she could have said herself, and that surprised her, actually, since she was still a bit of a romantic at heart. Romantic at heart, maybe, but never again as an indulger in romance. Even if her Prince Charming came riding into her life on his donkey she'd send him in the opposite direction. That was the lot of her life now. Time to accept it and run off the foolish notions. "I understand, totally. Mauricio wanted things that I was not, and couldn't be. And I wanted things that he wasn't. Only it took me an awfully long time to figure out that he wasn't going to change and neither was I, even though I clung to the hope of it for so long. But in my defense, part of that clinging was because of the clinic. Walking away from Mauricio meant walking away from the clinic, and I couldn't do that. Not at the time, anyway. So I suppose you could say Mauricio was the compromise I made to be able to do what I wanted to do." She chuckled. "Sounds pretty stupid when you say it aloud, doesn't it?"

"Not stupid at all. We all make compromises to get what we want. Yours was merely setting aside your personal needs for your professional passion. And I think that's pretty admirable. Lonely at night, but admirable."

"So, is Joanna happy now?" Mauricio was. Three weeks after she'd left him, he got himself engaged to a one of the nurses in the hospital they'd used, married her a month later, and produced Mauricio Junior nine months after that. A full circle for Mauricio, one that she could not have completed for him.

"Very. She's found the life she couldn't have with me."

And Mauricio found…well, definitely a life they hadn't had. "But staying here, you didn't get your fresh start the way she did when she left Kijé. Didn't you want that for yourself, too?"

"Oh, but I did get it. I get a fresh start every single day…every time I succeed in opening a new program, or raising enough money to fund an old one." He patted the donkey on the neck. "Meeting Gertie here is another fresh start."

"So, do you have any regrets, other than the fact that you don't have much of a chance to practice clinical medicine?"

"No regrets whatsoever. I'm one of the lucky ones who knows exactly where they're meant to be, and what they're meant to be doing. And you? Any regrets?"

None, unless she wanted to consider the fact that this brief acquaintance with Paul was most likely all she would ever have with him. Maybe they'd pass each other along the way once in a while. Perhaps make arrangements for a brief meeting to discuss various patients and practices. But that's all it could be, all that her life would allow. Which, surprisingly, was becoming a deep regret, one that truly shocked her, because with Paul she could see so much more than she might have chosen for herself. "No regrets whatsoever," she lied, trying to ignore a heavy-hearted shroud slipping down over her. "Not at all."

Solange glanced ahead, trying to focus on the journey and not these little longings that were starting to creep in. "Up ahead, where the road divides, we'll go to the right and start a gradual ascent into the foothills. The Mission is actually in the foothills and not the mountains. But by donkey, or on foot, foothills and mountains all seem about the same."

As it turned out, Gertie knew the way, and however hard Paul struggled to guide her turned out to be an annoyance to the beast because she brayed, then bucked and finally threw him off. Laughing, and actually glad for the momentary distraction from some impossible feelings trying to clog her thoughts, Solange scrambled off Pete and ran to him. "Are you OK?" she asked, extending a hand to help him up. "I should have warned you that she can be stubborn."

"Physically, I'll let you know in the morning if I'm OK, after the rest of my bruises have had a chance to come out." He got up, brushing the dust off himself with one hand and holding onto her hand with the other. And faking a scowl. But it wasn't long until the humor came sparkling right back into his eyes.

She'd already memorized it there, and counted on it. And dreamt about it the previous night. "I think Gertie's intention is to show you who's boss." He was holding onto her hand much too long, she thought, even though she made no attempt to pull away. It had been for ever since a man had touched her in any way, even Mauricio, and this little brush with Paul was setting off sparks she hadn't even known she had. Sparks she didn't believe Paul was feeling, as he was still rambling on and on about the donkey.

With a yearning sigh she was certain that he heard, Solange finally let go of Paul's hand and backed away from him. "You could always walk, and lead Gertie." She looked up at him, suddenly feeling self-conscious, like he could read all those confusing thoughts swirling around in her mind. "Maybe that'll save you from getting any more bruises."

"Bruises I can take." He chuckled. "But being outsmarted by a donkey I can't." He reached out and brushed his fingers across her cheek. "I make you uncomfortable, don't I, Solange?"

Solange glanced back down at the ground. "No, it's not you. It's…it's something I don't know how to explain." Or wouldn't explain. Not to him. "I don't have friends, Paul. Or relationships. Outside the people I work with, and the villagers I call on, I don't have…" She shrugged. "It's not my life."

Her eyes were still on the ground because she knew if she looked up right then he would be able to read things no one was meant to read. Longing and desire…things she'd put away a very long time ago, vowing never to let out again. And maybe there was more. Maybe she did have some fledgling feelings for Paul, something other than attraction on the purest physical level, the beginning of feelings she couldn't yet sort out, or didn't want to. Or maybe was afraid to. Paul was a perceptive man. He would see it all in her eyes if she looked up at him. So she wouldn't look.

"What is it you want, Solange?" he asked, slipping his hand under her chin to tilt her face up to his.

So many things, things he would never know. "Nothing ever changes with me, Paul. I want what I've always wanted. To do what's best for my patients. It's simple, and it's complicated, but it's what it always has been." And always would be.

"I think you want more. I think you want so many things you're denying yourself. But let me just say that you're an amazing woman, Solange Léandre. One who would be so easy to love, if I did that sort of thing any more." He put a finger to her lips to silence her budding protest. "But I don't, so don't worry. From the moment you entered your father's party I knew that I wanted to know you. And, yes, that was physical attraction, pure and simple. You're some great-looking lady, and I'm not denying that I noticed the physical thing first. Every single man in the room noticed you, in case you weren't aware of it. But who you are… My God, Solange! There aren't any words to fit what's going on inside me right now other than to say you're an amazing woman. One who *could* be so easy to love."

Solange brushed Paul's fingers away from her face. "We are who we are, dictated by what we do. It's a pure vision, Paul. But not always such an easy one, is it?" Maybe in a while, once Paul had returned to his life, and she to hers, she would come to realize it had all been innocent flirtation, or that finally, after a year, she was rebounding from Mauricio. Maybe she'd come to realize she enjoyed being with Paul like she'd enjoyed being with no one before. Including Mauricio.

It was starvation in a way she was just now coming to understand. But right now, to her, it felt like love. One thing was sure. Since she wasn't reining in her own emotions very well, at least she could count on Paul to keep a level head.

Grabbing a canteen off the donkey Lulu, Solange opened

it and took a drink, then handed it over to Paul. "Are you playing an angle with me, Paul?" she blurted, almost as surprised by her words as he appeared to be. But why was he here? In spite of what he'd told her, and in spite of her feelings, she did still wonder.

"Is that what you think?"

"I don't want to, but it's a possibility, because isn't that what you do, Paul? You play all the right angles in the hope of someone giving you a nice fat contribution? Do you not play the angles with my father in exchange for funds for your hospital?"

"Well, I'll admit that you do have some awfully nice angles, Solange." His mouth curved into a wide, boldly sexual smile just to show how much he admired those angles. "But I'm not playing one with you, because, to be honest, you don't have anything that will benefit me. You're not so connected to your father that he'll up his contributions to me, if that's what you think this is about."

"It did occur to me." Shaking her head skeptically, she walked back over to her donkey. "Everybody wants something, Paul. I know I do. So you can't fault me for wondering what it is that you expect by coming along with me. Especially since time spent with me is time spent away from your efforts."

The hope of a one-night stand wasn't it, she didn't believe. He was a handsome, charming man who could have any woman he wanted—a thought that did sting a bit. So, was this the ultimate act of altruism for him, coming to her rescue? Was she the damsel in distress appealing to his knight-in-shining-armor fantasy?

Certainly, there had to be more to it than met the eye, because Paul wouldn't be out here right now, risking donkey and tropical storm, simply to tag along.

Or would he? "In other words, you're not going to tell me why you're doing this?"

"Like I said, Frère Léon..." He winked at her, then turned his attention to Gertie, holding out a piece of candy to her.

"One piece of candy and you charm the world. You're good, Paul." She laughed. "And calculating, I think." And sexy as hell, with that roguish twinkle in his eyes. Too bad they couldn't go about this flirtation for real.

"Is it so hard for you to believe that I would go through all this without this great ulterior motive you seem to think I have?"

"Everybody wants something, city boy. That's the way the world works."

Paul hoisted himself up on the donkey's back, then looked down at Solange. "Sometimes it's not an angle, Solange. Sometimes it's a reason. And those of us who don't have angles do have our reasons."

Gertie gave a snort, then began her slow, deliberate pace along the trail as Solange hung back on Pete, trying to figure out what to make of this—of Paul, of herself, of her feelings for him.

She glanced up at the sky again, frowning. Suddenly, the complication of a tropical storm seemed the least of all her complications, because she caught herself hoping that his only tag-along reason was to spend more time with her. And that was an unexpected desire that came with a *huge* complication.

Paul wanted to glance over his shoulder at her. More like he was fighting to stop himself from glancing back at her. He knew she was lagging back, and he couldn't blame her for that. *Could* be easy to love... What was that all about, anyway? She was *definitely* easy to love, and he was pretty sure he did in some bedeviling variation, or at least he was headed in that direction, and not able to hold back. She didn't want the tangle, though, and that was patently obvious. He certainly didn't either, although he did seem to be tap-dancing around it a bit, didn't he? Was he inclined to chuck his well-rehearsed resolve? Yes... No... He wanted to, and he didn't want to, because the result was predictable. And a simple fling with Solange was out of the question because that would not be enough. Not nearly enough. A lifetime wouldn't be enough. And he didn't do lifetimes. Couldn't.

So possibly the easiest thing to do was admit that he was here because he wanted to spend time with her, then let her send him away since she wouldn't, or couldn't, reciprocate. Angle...reason...both the same. He wanted to get to know her, even when every sensible corpuscle inside him knew that he shouldn't. But it wasn't those sensible corpuscles winning this round, was it?

"Don't think we're going to make it to wherever we're going before the rain starts," he called back to her. Not that it mattered, when at the end of this trail, wet or dry, he'd be with Solange. Right here, right now, that's all that counted. He'd figure out the rest of it later on.

The first splashes of rain were slight. Simply a few big, fat drops in warning. Then the wind picked up, but not so much that it was anything to worry about. Not yet. "Paul," she shouted above the wind. "You're going to see a trail veering off the path in just another minute. Take it. We need to get to the village and find shelter there until this blows over."

He twisted around and waved. "Think we'll make it before all hell breaks loose?"

"It's going to be close." A gust of wind caught her and shoved her off balance. Clinging to Pete, she righted herself, then looked back to make sure Lulu's cargo was still tied securely.

"You OK?" Paul shouted.

"Fine." But getting a little nervous. This storm was blowing in hard and fast and Gertie, in her ever-slow pace, wasn't going to be rushed into anything, meaning they were still ten minutes from safety. Ten minutes and the rain was already picking up. So was the wind. "We have to walk in," she yelled. "Get off Gertie and lead her." As she said that, she slid off Pete's back and took him by the reins. They would keep better pace that way.

She didn't say a word for the next several minutes as she pulled up close to Paul and followed him along the path. At the turn-off, he stopped and turned around. The wind was blowing against them now, getting harder with every passing second. Luckily, the rain was steady, but not ferocious. "How about you run on ahead and I'll lead the donkeys in? No sense having both of us knocked about in all this." He raised his hand to his face to wipe the rain from his eyes, then pushed his wet hair back. "You can get us a nice, cozy lodge. Have a fire started in the fireplace when I get there, call room service."

"How about you doing that while I lead the animals in?" she countered.

"Are you always this stubborn?" he shouted over the howling wind.

Solange ducked her head to avoid the rain and, like Paul, pushed her wet hair back from her eyes. That's when she noticed that her totally soaked white T-shirt was nearly transparent, giving Paul a show he was thoroughly enjoying, impending storm or not. Not that she could do anything about it now. "Not stubborn. *Practical.* I'm better with the donkeys." She hunched forward a little, as if that would conceal what Paul had already been ogling. And not too bashfully at that.

"Then we'll just stick together like we've been doing. OK?"

Before Solange could answer, Paul pulled off his own shirt, a dark cotton one that wouldn't go transparent in the rain, and handed it to her. "I'd offer you the dry one from my pack, but I think we're going to need our dry clothes later on."

"Thank you, but I'm fine." She tried handing it back to him, but he refused.

"Allow me my moment of chivalry this one time, will you?"

She nodded as she pulled on the shirt, grateful for the gesture. Above everything else Paul was a gentleman, and she liked that. Yet there was the fact that his list of estimable qualities, which just kept getting longer all the time, was making it tougher on her to keep the objective in mind. "I *am* going to take the lead, though," she said. "See if I can get Gertie moving faster than you've got her doing."

His shirt was huge on her, so huge she took a quick look at his bare chest. Beautiful chest. Muscular, tanned, a nice matting of brown hair all wet and plastered to his body. It was an odd sensation, seeing him like that. Something caught between longing and anticipation—*and disappointment.* Well, it was good to know the hormones still worked. She hadn't been sure they would. "Thank you," she said, slipping past him to take her place with Gertie.

Gertie did pick up her pace with Solange, and as they made their way along the narrowing road, Solange was almost glad for the storm because it kept her mind off things she wanted desperately to think about, and knew she should not.

CHAPTER SIX

THE village's guest house was small and bare, with barely enough room inside for a man, a woman and three donkeys. Thatched roof, wooden floors, open doorway—it was a relatively dry place, with only a couple of leaky spots in the roof, and Étoué Babin, the village leader, offered Solange and Paul the use of several clay pots to catch the drips, while his young son, Ràfer, spread woven mats on the wooden floor for their comfort and placed a basket of fruit and freshly baked flat bread in a dry corner away from the donkeys.

Solange loved this place, loved the village, the house and the people. Generosity abounded, and everything they had was shared, even with total strangers. What the village lacked in modern conveniences it made up for in hospitality, and she always looked forward to traveling through, often spending a little longer there than she did many of her other routine stops. "They're good people," she said, ripping two pieces of bread from the flat disk, and handing one to Paul. "Sometimes I like coming here just for peace of mind."

"What's your day like? When you come here, what do you do?"

"I wait for them to come to me. If they have a need they

will. They understand what I do, and respect it. And I respect them enough not to push myself on them. There's a fine line out here in the way you dispense your medicine, and, as nice as the people are, if you cross that line you'll offend them, which will undo everything. So I sit here in the visitors' quarters for an hour and wait. Then if no one comes to me, I leave."

"Do they come?" he asked.

"Always. And they're getting less and less shy about it. I'm betting within in the next ten minutes, storm notwithstanding, there will be a line outside."

"And what are the common complaints? What types of conditions do you normally see?"

"Pretty much the same things I saw in Miami and Chicago. Infections of various sorts, stomachaches, headaches, menstrual complaints. I don't have anyone here with TB, like I do in a couple of the other villages, although I'm going to send Louise Babin down to you shortly to have a sed rate done because I think she has an early onset of rheumatoid arthritis in her hands, and if that's the case I want to get her started on some non-steroidal anti-inflammatories right away."

"Send her down any time. We'll get the sed rate done, and how about X-rays to see what kinds of orthopedic changes she might be experiencing? Something to use as a baseline for the future."

"I'd appreciate that. I talked to Bijou and she said that the middle of the week is the best time for lab tests that aren't urgent, so I'll see if Frère Léon will be free to drive Louise. I think he's going to be my shuttle service much of the time."

Frère Léon to the rescue. He was the one who had brought Paul and her together, and hopefully the one who would stay between them. With her fly-away, weak-willed attitudes lately, she was counting on that.

Paul sat down next to Solange in the doorway, and immediately she sprang up and went back to the basket with the fruit and bread. It was a pretense, to get away from him. He recognized that. And he wasn't going to point it out to her because it was her choice, her life, and she called the shots regarding it. So now he was sitting there alone, still bare-chested, still wet, with Gertie, not Solange, nudging him in the back.

Certainly in the span of twenty-four hours he hadn't succeeded very well as far as Solange was concerned. Just when he thought they might be friends, she pulled back. Was she afraid? Maybe afraid that a rainy afternoon in a guest house might lead to more than idle conversation? Or maybe she was simply afraid of him. "Do you hate men?" he asked bluntly.

She blinked in surprise. "What makes you think that I hate men?"

"Just a hunch. Relationship gone bad and now..." He shrugged. "And now you hide in the corner instead of sitting down next to me. I'm not a psychiatrist, but I'd say that was a pretty good indication of some kind of emotion going on."

"I don't get involved," she said. "That's all it is. I don't, I won't, and when something starts, as Allain would say, *quacking* like a relationship, I get up and stand in the corner. It's nothing personal, really."

"And you're afraid that's what this is? The beginning of some kind of relationship between us."

"Isn't it?"

"It could be, I'll admit. Except I don't do what you don't

do. Different reason, same outcome." Paul patted the floor next to him. "Friends?"

"Paul, there are so many things you don't know about me...things that I just can't..." She walked slowly back to the doorway and sat down next to him.

"You don't have to, Solange. Whatever it is, you don't have to talk about it, and I won't pry."

"It took me a long time to get to this place in my life, Paul. I don't want to leave, and I'm scared to death of changes."

"Nobody's asking you to leave, and I would never expect you to change. Not in any way."

"Friends," she said affirmatively. "That all we can be."

Sighing wistfully, a deep regret was beginning to seep into his pores that he hadn't met Solange Léandre at another time in his life. Every fiber of his being told him it could have been good...*would* have been good. "I respect that." He respected it because he understood it.

So, as Paul reconciled himself to the way he would spend his late afternoon, sitting amongst the donkeys, waiting for the rain to stop, thinking about Solange, trying to fit together all the pieces of her that he'd gathered up, she reached across and slipped her hand into his. So unexpected, and so shy. And so delicately, as he would expect from Solange. The hand of a friend, if that's all she would allow him.

He took her hand and held it gently, even though to him it felt more like a lifeline to which he wanted to cling. Then they watched the rain together.

"It's so nice when it's quiet like this," she said. "Quiet and gentle. Solaina and I played outside in the rain sometimes, when Papa wasn't around. We had a swimming pool, and we weren't far away from the beach. But the rain was different. Special." It was so good to get off the subject of uncertainties. And that's what their relationship was—a big uncertainty. She liked it better when they stayed in the moment. Like now. All they had was the moment, so why waste it?

"Where is she...your sister?"

"She's living in a little country called Dharavaj. Originally she went there to work in the hospital as the director of nursing. Then she went to a clinic to brush up on her nursing skills. Now she's settling into practice as a nurse in a little hospital with her new husband."

"And she's happy there?"

"Happier than she's ever been. But I think it has more to do with her husband than anything else. So what about you, Paul? Brothers, sisters?"

"Only child. No one to play with in the rain. But I never minded playing alone. And my family life was pretty typical of the average American family, I think. We weren't wealthy. We didn't travel, except to visit family. My mother had a part-time job, and was at home to greet me every day after school. My father was a doctor. A country GP. Simple man, simple medical practice, and always happy."

"Was?"

"He died when I was away in medical school. Never got to see me complete it."

"And that makes you sad, doesn't it?"

"It did, because who I was when he died wasn't who I finally became. And he would have liked me much better now. I think he probably knew what kind of a man I'd become when I finally let myself do it. He was smart like that. Insightful. Always my example. Kind, generous...he didn't turn people away if they couldn't pay for his services. If they needed medical treatment and had only a dozen fresh eggs to offer in payment, he'd take the eggs and we'd have omelets for supper." Paul chuckled. "And trust me, early in my career it was never my intention to take eggs in payment for anything. I wanted the opposite of what my dad had, because I mistakenly thought it was wrong to work so hard and spend your life with so little the way he did. But now my biggest regret, I think, is that he never saw me once I was through with all the grandiose ideas."

Such a nice, normal family. She envied him that. The way she and Solaina had traveled back and forth when they had been children, never staying in one place more than a month or two...she would have loved the stability. That was then, however. Now she was on the move constantly, and it suited her. A legitimate reason to keep running away... "He would have been proud, Paul. You've carried out his legacy quite nicely, chicken eggs or not. And I think that somehow he knows that."

"That's kind of you to say."

"And your mother?"

"She sells real estate. Very good at it. Just last month she was the top in sales in her company."

"So you've inherited the best of both your parents."

"Funny how that worked out, isn't it? I always knew I was going to be some kind of a doctor. Never knew I would actually be a better salesman."

"You're a good doctor, too." This would have been a good afternoon to cozy up in bed with him, read the newspaper together, sip tea, make love. It wasn't often that she missed the life where she could do that, but today she did miss it. Sadly, the closest they were going to get to anything like it was this, sitting in the open doorway, dangling their feet outside and watching the rain splash into puddles on the ground.

It was good, though. The nicest afternoon she'd had since she couldn't remember when. "Thank you," she said wistfully.

"For what?"

"For being here."

Paul turned over the little girl's hand and looked at the tiny scratch on her thumb. Then he squatted down so he was eye to eye with her. "Looks to me like you'll need a bandage," he said.

Her wide brown eyes weren't frightened so much as hesitant. It had taken great courage for little Ghislaine to come to them, and Paul was doing splendidly with her. Ghislaine didn't understand him, neither did he understand Ghislaine. But the body language between them was obvious, and warm.

"You're good with children," Solange said, handing him a tube of ointment and a bandage.

He smiled at Ghislaine as he answered Solange. "I've always loved children, and once, a long time ago, I considered going into pediatrics, but I got sidetracked into infectious diseases."

"And you and Joanna didn't have children?" Funny how she'd never considered that. Paul, as a father. Seeing him with Ghislaine, it made perfect sense because he'd be a wonderful father.

"We talked about it at the start. I wanted a dozen, and she wanted…well, with me, none. She was all career…"

"And there's something wrong with that?" Solange snapped. "A woman wanting a career?"

"You've had this argument before, haven't you? With Mauricio?"

"Didn't mean to be so snappish," she said. This was Paul. He hadn't done anything to deserve that, after all. "But Mauricio did want children eventually, and I wanted...what I got."

"There's nothing wrong with a woman wanting her career, but Joanna should have been honest with me at the start. And who knows? If we'd had a child the outcome might have been different between us. But we didn't and it wasn't. Of course, she found the man she truly loves and now she has two children. So, as it turns out, it was me she didn't want, not the children."

"Regrets?"

"No, not really. I'd still love to be a father. Every man wants his legacy carried on, doesn't he? But it's not a practical idea with me away from home so often. Maybe someday..." He dabbed a spot of antibiotic ointment on Ghislaine's scratch, then covered it with a bandage. Before she left the guest house, he fished a piece of candy from his pocket and handed it to her. Then, within two minutes, every child in the village was lined up at the door, awaiting their examinations.

"Looks like you've really stirred things up here." Solange laughed, dumping candy out of her pack into a bowl. "The children are usually more apprehensive. I think, Dr Killian, you are a natural with them. Papa Paul, perhaps."

"To your Maman Solange? I'd be honored,"

No more injuries were apparent in the children, and by the time all the candy was passed out, Louise Babin was standing outside, waving at her.

"I think you're being summoned," Paul commented, standing back up. "Need any help?"

Solange shook her head. "She's shy around men. I'll be

fine." She ducked out the door and he watched her until she disappeared into the Babin hut, then he sat back down in the doorway.

"I don't understand you, Solange," he whispered. "Don't even come close to understanding you." Even so, the feelings churning around in him didn't need that full understanding. They were for Solange, as she was.

"*Doktè!*" a woman from across the compound screamed.

Paul glanced around to see her frantically waving at him with one hand, grasping an infant to her chest with the other. He jumped up.

Slipping and sliding through the mud, Paul held his breath, fearing that the baby was the one he would see sick, judging from the way the woman was acting...pacing around in small circles until he reached her. The she broke into a rush of Creole, which he didn't understand. So he reached out to take the baby from her arms so he could have a look, but she slapped at his hands, stepped back, and launched into another, more frantic outburst of Creole.

"I don't understand," he said simply, trying to steer himself into a view from which he could have a speedy little glance-over of the child, but she merely snatched the baby out of his sight.

Finally, when the woman was sufficiently convinced that Paul wouldn't advance improperly upon her once her back was turned to him, she gestured for him to follow. Which he did, to the edge of the village and on through a little thicket of vegetation where a scruffy nanny goat was caught up in a clump of branches, kicking, pulling and crying desperately to free herself.

"A goat?" He chuckled. Solange was off doing something

as noble as taking care of a woman with rheumatoid arthritis, and his patient was a prickly goat caught up in a patch of brambles. "Why not?" he quipped, approaching the choleric beast. She was pawing the ground now, and if not for the fact Paul absolutely knew that goats didn't breathe fire, he would have sworn he saw smoke streaming from her nostrils. Death by she-goat. Not a fitting obituary, even for a city boy. Solange would find the irony, and humor, in that, he supposed.

Paul took a couple of steps forward, then the goat screamed. She screamed again as he took a few more steps. Behind him, he could hear a small crowd gathering. Probably to laugh at him. But who could blame them? He'd be laughing, too, watching himself go after a goat. "OK," he said to the beast as he got closer, "make me look like a hero here, will you? And be gentle with me."

At his words, the goat tilted her head in curiosity, then stretched out her neck to Paul's pants pocket as he stepped alongside her. Smelling the candy apparently, she rolled up her lips, grabbed hold of the pocket and ripped the fabric away before Paul could push her aside. Once the fabric was torn, the goat nosed right on in for her treats. In that instant Paul cleared away the brambles, then took a step back. The goat went right with him, determined to have a look in his other pocket. "No, you don't..." he said, still backing away. When he was several paces away from the animal, he turned to the woman who'd asked for his help, and as he did that, several people in the crowd yelled and pointed at the persistent nanny, who now had her head lowered and seemed to be taking aim on her target...Paul.

"Great," he muttered, as the beast start her charge. Paul's immediate reaction was to turn and run, but two of the villagers stepped out, grabbed the goat and tied a rope around her neck. Then the incident was over and both goat and rescuer walked away unscathed.

Quickly, he looked to see if Solange had watched any of his failure at goat herding, but thankfully she was nowhere to be seen. It was amazing how, even in the small things, what Solange thought about him mattered so much. "Maybe it's the challenge," he said aloud, since no one was there to listen. "The more she doesn't want me, the more I want to be wanted."

Halfway back to the village, Paul heard soft, frantic cries coming from somewhere nearby. He whipped around, surveying the area around him, but saw no one. "Hello," he shouted.

The muffled cries grew louder. Definitely *not* another goat.

"Please, let me help you," he called, even though he knew whoever was out there probably couldn't understand him. But maybe by the tone of his voice… "Tell me where you are and I'll come get you."

Still no answer, so Paul started walking in the direction from which he believed the sound was coming. First straight ahead, then to the right and to the left. It took a minute, but eventually he did find a woman lying underneath a tree in the mud, her face twisted in agony. She was a large woman, young, and very obviously unhappy over the fact that he was the one to find her. Had she not been propped with her back against the tree, she would have scooted backwards, completely away from him. *Like Solange, calling out then backing away when he answered.*

"My name is Paul," he said, walking slowly toward her, much the same way he'd approached the goat—cautiously. "Doktè Paul. My name is Doktè Paul." As if that meant anything to the woman.

She recoiled as he drew closer, and shook her head, then closed her eyes so she wouldn't have to look at him.

"I'm here to help you, and I promise that I won't hurt you," he said, trying to make his voice sound as gentle as possible. But the reality was, no matter how he sounded, the woman was afraid of him. Scared to death, actually, judging by the way she was shaking.

Knowing that, he could go no closer. "Look, I'm going back to get Solange."

She opened her eyes at the mention of Solange's name, and pointed to her left shoulder.

"You've hurt your shoulder?" He nodded, smiling. "I'll be right back." And he was, two minutes later, with Solange right behind him. "I'm not sure what's wrong with her. I couldn't get close enough to have a look, but I'm betting she might have dislocated her shoulder, judging from the way she's favoring it."

Solange bent down in front of the woman, said a few words, probed the tender area, then nodded her agreement after her quick examination. "She slipped in the mud and fell on it. And I think you're correct about it—it's dislocated. An X-ray would be nice right about now, but since we don't have one…" Her voice trailed off as she laid her hand gently across the woman's and gave it an encouraging squeeze.

"Since we don't have one," Paul supplied, "we'll take care of it ourselves. Do a reduction." He winced, thinking how painful that could be. But there wasn't another choice, and this was one fix that would be quick and effective. What was so painful for the woman now would be virtually pain-free in another minute or two.

Without discussing what to do between them, Solange instructed the woman, called Doucet, to stand, then bend at the waist. Solange supported her at the chest while Paul took hold of Doucet's wrist. "Tell her I'm going to pull down on it then rotate it, and that it might hurt."

"I already did," Solange said.

"Reading my mind?"

"No. Just anticipating you." She smiled at him. "And Doucet said to tell you that you did a good job rescuing the goat, and now she trusts you to take care of her because of that."

"Saved by the goat?"

As he spoke, Paul applied steady, downward traction then an external rotation to Doucet's arm. "I missed the day they went over goat rescue in medical school. Pity, because these were my favorite pants." While maintaining traction, he began to flex Doucet's shoulder as Solange applied thumb pressure to Doucet's scapula. Next, Paul rotated the woman's shoulder, and within seconds there was a little pop, the one that meant the shoulder joint was back in its proper place.

"We do good work together, Doctor," Solange commented, helping Doucet stand back up. She took a few seconds to explain to their patient how to favor that arm for a couple of days, then sent her on her way.

"Just keep in mind that I was the one she wouldn't let come near her."

"Because she's never seen a white man before. Not because she sensed you were a bad doctor. And as I said, she did admire your goat skills."

As Paul tried to step around Solange, she blocked his path, smiling. "So did I, Paul. Your goat skills, and your skills with the villagers, are very good. And the children here adore you.

They can't wait for Doktè Candy, as they're calling you now, to return."

She was standing so close to him he could feel the warmth from her body, smell the antiseptic of the handwash she'd used before she'd treated her patient. And, yes, those little jolts of electricity arcing back and forth between them…

This was the point where he should have kissed her. In a movie, he would have pulled her into his arms and to hell with everything else they had to contend with. The kiss…that magical moment where full awareness should dawn…the kiss that would not happen.

But he couldn't do that. And he wouldn't, no matter how much the moment called for it, no matter how much he wanted to feel her lips pressed to his, to feel her desire as he was feeling his own right now.

The call would be Solange's. It had to be. And he had no idea if she would make it.

CHAPTER SEVEN

"I KNOW you're probably going to argue with me over this, Paul, but I'm going back to my infirmary tonight. It's another hour from here, maybe two, because it's going to be a tough hike from all the rain making the trail muddy. But I'm going to try it."

"Does it make that much difference?" he asked. "One more night away?"

"Probably not. Except I've got open clinic in the morning, meaning people will be trooping in from all over. And most likely a good many of them are already there. They tend to do that—come in the night before and camp out."

"But I thought you traveled out to them."

"I do. But I also have set days when they know they can come to me, since I don't make it to every region as often as I would like. I'll be at the infirmary for a day, then I'll go back out for two. Then I'll come back for a day, and go out for three."

"And in an emergency?"

"Ayida and Keskeya always know where I am, and Frère Léon has a relay system of sorts set up. Word travels fast up here." She laughed. "You'd be surprised how fast."

"It sounds like you're prepared for just about every contingency."

"Except getting you up the mountain in the dark in the mud. It's a tough hike, Paul." Solange grabbed up her packs from the floor, slung one over her shoulder and carried the other in her hand. "It's better this way. When I catch up to Frère Léon, I'll have him bring Louise down for her tests, and you can do your yearly physical on him at that time, if you're there. If not, he'll catch up to you at some point because he'll be the one bringing the villagers in for any test I prescribe, so you two will eventually run into each other."

She didn't want to leave him, but she did have to walk away from him some time, and this was as good a time as any to do it. Before anything happened between them. She could read it in his eyes, and she was sure he could read it in hers. So why keep testing fate? Why keep tempting each other? Call it back in, then walk away.

It was for the best. For Paul's best.

"And if I follow you?" he asked, stepping into the door opening, completely blocking it with his massive form.

"If you follow me, I can't stop you. But I'm asking you not to, Paul. There's no point." She ran her toe across the dusty floorboards and marked a line. "We're divided, and we have to stay that way. You on your side, me on mine, and we've been coming too close to the line. But that won't work in your life. And it won't work in mine. So this is as close as it comes for us. Toe to the line, and no further. But if it's of any consolation, if ever there was a man worth crossing the line for…"

She leaned up and bushed a kiss to his lips. Soft and gentle, and it roused such a heat in her so quickly, she stepped back and did not look up at him. "I got carried away. You coming back with me, a nice afternoon in the rain, even the lobster...it shouldn't have happened. That made it personal, and this cannot be personal. My life doesn't have room for personal."

"I won't force myself on you, Solange. Not in any way."

"It's for the best," she said, trying not to allow despondency to show through her voice. Such a perfect afternoon ending like this. How could she feel anything else?

"Is it?"

"Yes." For Paul, it was. And since she was already used to making the sacrifices, he was just one more sacrifice for her. Pure and simple. One more on her list. And she wanted desperately to be pragmatic about that, but there was nothing at all pragmatic about the way her heart was aching.

Solange reached up and brushed her hand across his cheek. Earlier, he had told her she could be easy to love. Such cherished words...words she would never forget because they had come from a man who *was* so easy to love. And she *was* in love with him. As silly as it might seem, and for as little time as she'd known him, everything about Paul Killian had made her fall in love with him. More and more each passing moment. So now she had to protect her heart. *And him.* "Thank you for everything," she murmured, then slipped through the door and into the night.

The hike back to The Mission took a little less than two hours, and by the time Solange arrived she was exhausted, physically and emotionally. *And she was beginning to feel that old frailty setting in again.* One she didn't want to come back. One she was very grateful Paul hadn't seen. In her emotions, in her physical actions...it caught her in times she didn't expect it to, and dragged her down when she could least afford it. Hard work, long hours. Exhausting to anyone on a normal schedule, and nothing about her schedule was normal.

Whatever the case, as Solange tumbled into her own little bed in her own little room, she was glad to be there. Sleep. That's all she needed, and in the morning she would feel much better. She always did. "Alone," she murmured, as she pulled the mosquito netting into place around her for the first time in ever so long, she truly wished she wasn't alone.

"Maman Solange! Maman Solange!"

"Let me sleep," she begged. It had been only a few minutes, and tonight she needed more than that.

"Maman Solange!" the young voice persisted. Chanté, she thought. Ayida's granddaughter.

"No," Solange mumbled, fighting to stay asleep. "Maman is tired. *Très fatiguée.* You go tell your *grandmère* to wake me up first thing in the morning."

"It's afternoon," Keskeya said, shuffling over to Solange. Keskeya Volcy, a young woman with a club foot that slowed her down, and a heart of gold that never failed her, was not a trained nurse, but, then, neither was Ayida. Solange couldn't run the infirmary without them, though. "And Frère Léon has been fussing all over the place about the line of people out there waiting for you."

"*Mon Dieu!*" Solange exclaimed, jumping up. Clinic day! "Why didn't somebody come and wake me up?"

"Because he told us not to."

"Frère Léon told you not to wake me up?"

"No! Frère Léon wanted to wake you up hours ago, but the other one wouldn't let him. The kiddies call him Doktè Candy because he tosses candy out to him."

"Paul's here?"

"If you mean that handsome white man with the blue eyes out there, yes, he's here. And he's seeing all those people who expected to see you."

Solange drew in a deep breath. "Paul's taken over my infirmary?"

"Somebody had to do it, as you were all set to sleep the whole day away. If you ask me, that man is a blessing to us. Don't know where you found him, but I sure hope you don't send him back where he came from because he's got things better taken care of than you do."

A heart of gold and a very blunt tongue. Solange laughed. She loved Keskeya. "I'll take a shower and be over to the infirmary in ten minutes."

"Are you getting down in the womanly way again?" Keskeya asked, her face twisting into genuine concern. "That happens when you don't take care of yourself, you know. It comes back on you and your body can't be taking much more of that punishment."

"There's nothing coming back on me," Solange snapped, then instantly regretted it. Keskeya was concerned, and Solange appreciated that. But the *womanly thing*, as her dear friend called it, was still a touchy matter. At thirty-one, no woman ever expected to have her uterus and ovaries ripped out of her, but that's what had happened. A few swipes of the gynecologist's knife and her life had changed for ever. "I'm just tired. Off my regular schedule." Falling in love without the hope of a chance to act on it. "But I'm fine now."

"Maybe your Doktè Paul should have a look at you. He seems competent, *for a man*." Keskeya laughed. "Bet you've been noticing that all the time you were gone, weren't you?"

Precisely the problem, Solange thought. And now Paul was having such a distracting effect on her that her work was suffering. "I'm fine," she insisted again.

"You may think you're fine, but you're not, and the last person to have an appointment with a *doktè* is a *doktè*." Keskeya snorted. "That makes no good sense to me!"

"I have a perfectly good doctor."

"In Miami. And how long since you've been in Miami?" Keskeya stepped away, then turned back for one final retort. "You need to get your blood levels checked and get those drugs readjusted, and you know that. Don't take no doctor to prescribe that."

"What am I going to do, *maman*?" Solange whispered, on the verge of tears, after Keskeya left the room. Keskeya was right to a certain point. Something *was* coming back on her, but it wasn't the so-called womanly thing over her hysterectomy and hormones, unless falling in love and knowing it could never be was considered womanly. Their schedules didn't permit it, and even if they had, Paul wanted children. *He needed children.* At his age, he expected children. "What do I tell him, *maman*? 'Here I am, the one doesn't have a son or daughter to bear for you?' What do I tell him, maman?"

She didn't wait long for an answer because there was no time to waste fretting over things that could never be. She had patients to see. Swiping at a stray tear sliding down her cheek, Solange drew in a deep, resolute breath and grabbed a handful of clean clothes out of a bureau drawer. Then she headed out the door to the shower across the hall, thinking about everything she had, and not what she couldn't have.

The Mission…lovely work here. She loved it. And the chapel. The accommodations were splendid—several small sleeping rooms up and down both sides of the structure, a commons area in the center where they took their meals, watched television when the satellite was pointed in the right direction, a retrofit of modern and semi-modern kitchen and bathing facilities... This was a wonderful place, a tremendous situation. That's what she had to think about.

Not completely over her momentary regret over what she couldn't have, but becoming more heartened the harder she thought about what she *did* have, Solange ducked in and out of the shower in record time, even for her, dried off and headed straight to the infirmary, where there was still a considerable line outside, men, women and children all waiting their turns.

"Your friend gave the children a hacky sack," Ayida said, as she scurried by with a baby in her arms.

"What's a hacky sack?" Solange asked.

Keskeya smiled, coming to Solange's side. "A little cloth bag of beans that they kick to each other with their knees. I thought it was such a waste of good beans, but the children already love it as a toy, and that man of yours has brought all kinds of hacky sacks with him." She pointed to several small groups of children playing in the commons. "It takes up their time while their parents see the *doktè*."

"He's not my man," Solange protested, against a force she knew would never give in. Keskeya had made up her mind, and it wouldn't be changed. But Solange somehow felt obligated to make her position in this matter public, if Ayida and Keskeya could be considered public.

"Ha!" Keskeya snorted. "You tell the lie as poorly as you look."

In response, Solange merely shook her head and walked away. No use arguing. No time for it, anyway.

"I knew you two would hit it off splendidly!" Frère Léon called from across the compound, where he was playing hacky sack with a group of younger kiddies. Short, chubby, balding, and true to his vocation in his long, brown robe, he was a man of seventy, or somewhere close to it, with the spunk of someone half his age. He came from a French monastic order that had been in the islands for well over a century now, delivering humanitarian aid wherever it was needed. The first time she'd met Frère Léon had been shortly after her mother had performed open heart surgery on him. After that, for years he kept popping back into her life at odd times, but mostly at times when she needed him, and she loved him dearly.

Instead of responding, she waved him off and continued toward the infirmary, where a dozen people were waiting patiently outside. "Are you expecting me to thank you for your interference?" she snapped at Paul as she entered the small building. He was helping an elderly man down off the exam table, a man who was beaming from ear to ear and lavishing Paul with profuse thanks.

"Stomachache," Paul said, ignoring her outburst. "A week in duration now."

"Ulcer?" she asked, suddenly forgetting her impatience with Paul.

"Ti-Malice," Paul answered, then grinned. "With every meal. I think it finally burned right through his stomach. He's promised to cut back to one meal a day using the Ti-Malice he normally makes. Or switch the pepper in his usual recipe to one not so hot. His choice, and he'll be back to see you in a couple of weeks." Ti-Malice—a diabolically hot sauce many islanders loved on their food. Hubert Aubin apparently loved it more than most, but the love affair was now waning, at least in the Ti-Malice's love for Hubert, although not in his love for the Ti-Malice.

Paul handed Hubert a bottle of generic antacids and sent him on his way. "So, are you feeling better?" he asked, once the office was empty. "Ayida and Keskeya said you were awfully tired."

"So you let me sleep late!" she snapped.

"Actually, I didn't *let* you do anything. You slept late because you needed it, and I did nothing to stop you. You can't have it both ways, Solange. Either I get to interfere, or I don't. Since I'd assumed your preference was no interference, I didn't." He stepped over to the tiny sink to wash his hands. "And before you snap my head off about coming here against your wishes, you're not the only person involved here. I wanted to have a short visit with Frère Léon, too."

"And stand in for me, while you conveniently *didn't* interfere with my over-sleeping."

Paul spun around to Solange, then took a few steps toward her before she thrust out her hand to stop him. "Are you OK?" he asked. "Keskeya says you're feeling poorly, and she asked me if I would take a look at you."

"What else did she say?" Solange hissed, sucking in a sharp breath. Paul wasn't to know. Beside Ayida, Keskeya and Frère Léon, no one was to know. People looked at you oddly when they knew you were barren at such a young age. *Poor Solange, she would have made a wonderful mother. There's always adoption. You still have your work.* And Mauricio had looked at her with such revulsion when the news had been give to him. He'd wanted his woman intact—womb, ovaries and hormones. Ready to make babies for him.

She couldn't bear to see that look in Paul's eyes.

"Nothing, except that she's worried."

He wasn't lying. Paul didn't have it in him to lie, which meant he didn't know. For that, she was relieved. "I'm just tired. It catches up to me sometimes, I suppose. And I'm sorry for being so grumpy, but I don't like shirking my responsibilities and expecting someone to make up for my shortfall."

"Being tired isn't a shortfall, Solange. It's natural. And I'm rather enjoying stepping back into a general practice for a little while. Even if my most difficult diagnosis of the day was hot sauce." He grinned. "So, shall we do the rest of this together, or do you want me to leave?"

"I'd love to do the rest of this together," she said, "if you don't mind working here. We don't have the facilities you do, as you've already noticed."

He walked the remaining steps to Solange, then pulled her into his arms. She started to protest, to pull away, but gave it a second thought and stayed there for a minute, just letting herself enjoy the feel of him. It was nice, and she would have stayed there much longer but there was work to do, and the work always came first. For both of them. "We've got at least a dozen more out there," she said, pulling away. "And I'm sure you'd like to get done here so you can have a nice chat with Frère Léon before you leave."

"Sounds like you're pushing me away."

"Just what the doctor prescribed."

"Which doctor?" he asked. "Because there are two in the room, and I know for a fact that one of them isn't prescribing."

* * *

"Where is he?" Solange asked, grabbing a gown and a mask.

"He's sitting under a tree right now, watching the others play hacky sack," Frère Léon said. "I know I should have brought him in straight way, but he wanted so badly to play with the other children, and I thought that a few minutes of fresh air, watching, might do him a spot of good, poor boy."

"How long has he been showing the symptoms?"

"Last time I was through his village he seemed fine. That was two weeks ago. I thought he'd lost a little weight, but he's getting taller now, so maybe that means thinner, too." He patted his ample belly, smiling. "Since I've never been thin, I don't know how those things work. But besides looking a little thin, Tsombé seemed as bright was usual."

Tsombé Patchou, age twelve. Solange suspected TB, and, judging from the look on Paul's face, so did he.

"I got him masked up good, and well away from the others," Frère Léon continued. "He's only been here a few minutes, and he's so enjoying himself, just watching."

"But you say he's feverish?"

"When his parents left him here, they said he'd been burning with the fever for three days now. Not eating. Bad cough rattling around in his chest, and I did hear that for sure. Even through his mask."

"Probably TB, and I'm going to act accordingly until we know otherwise." She glanced out of the door and saw Paul squatting under the tree where Tsombé was resting. "Are his parents still here?"

Frère Léon shook his head. "His father went off to work in the sugar cane, and his mother has other children. I told them we would take care of Tsombé, that they didn't have to worry. But I think his father will stop to see him in a few days."

Solange bent forward and gave Frère Léon a kiss on the cheek. "Have I told you lately how much I love you?"

"Save the sweet talk for Paul," he returned, blushing.

"So you are trying to play matchmaker. I suspected as much."

"When two people are so perfect for each other…" A broad grin crossed his chubby face. "What can I say? I may be celibate, but I'm still a romantic at heart."

"A romantic who knows my circumstances."

"The only circumstance I know is that you hide yourself behind your problems, and you make those problems for yourself because you still believe what that no-good Mauricio told you, that without *those* parts, you're no longer a woman. And the stupid man was a doctor. He should know better."

"Maybe I still hide a little, but I'm dealing with it much better now."

"You hid for a year at my little monastery. Locked yourself up in your cell when you weren't working in the infirmary or tending the garden, and dwelt in the past."

"Hormonal adjustments," she defended herself.

"Depression, hormonal adjustments, breakdown. All the same, when you spend a year in a monastery with a group of men who collectively didn't come close to looking at you the way Paul looks at you. It's in his eyes, Solange. The whole story, and all you have to do is look for it, because he very much wants to open those pages to you."

"Is that what he told you?"

"He told me he's through with relationships. That's all."

"And he means it." Which was just as well, as she was through with relationships, too. At least, the kind Frère Léon was trying to promote here.

"Then you would be perfect together since you've sworn off yourself." He gave her a kindly smile. "I know you're still having a bad time of it, Solange, but leave a little window open for a possibility. You deserve it."

"If you keep going on and on like that, I might have to give you another kiss."

"Save the kiss for Paul." He turned and trotted back to the hacky sack action, as Solange donned her mask, gown and gloves and headed out to Paul and Tsombé.

"Are you feeling better this afternoon?" she asked Tsombé, as she knelt down next to Paul. She'd seen him before, but only as she'd passed through his village. And he'd always seemed the picture of health. But this little boy...she was shocked. He'd grown very thin. And even without her stethoscope she could hear the gurgle of sounds from his chest. Even without the proper tests, she knew. So did Paul. It was obvious in the grim look he cast over the boy.

"Feeling OK," Tsombé said. His voice didn't sound OK, though. He sounded tired. Weak. Not the voice she remembered. "And I want to play hacky sack, too."

"What do you know about this hacky sack?" she asked, sitting down next to him.

"It's fun," he admitted, the eyes above his mask smiling. "And I want to play it with the others."

"Maybe in a few weeks," she promised, "after you've had a bit more rest. So, did you get a piece of candy?" she asked, pulling her stethoscope out of her pocket.

He opened his hand to show her the peppermint Paul had given him.

"He wants to play soccer," Paul said, pulling up Tsombé's shirt for Solange to have a listen. "I told him that I'm rather good at it, and that after he's well I might find a minute or two to give him a lesson." He winked at Solange. "He's got the legs of a soccer player, you know."

"And I expect the hacky sack will get him started in his responses," she said as she placed the bell of the stethoscope to the boy's chest. *Moist*. She could hear the fluid rattling around in there. Both lungs. Medically, the right lung was easier to treat than the left, but both Tsombé's lungs sounded bad. Pneumonia probably, or some other invasive infection. "Why don't you two plan some hacky sack strategy? I'll be right back, after I get some medicine." She looked at Paul. "Streptomycin for starters," she said. "And ethambutol." Streptomycin—an antibiotic, and ethambutol—a drug used help prevent those who already had TB from spreading it any further. "And I'm going to hold off on the INH until I get the proper diagnosis. No sense in overloading him at the start."

"I think maybe I'll take Tsombé back to my hospital tomorrow to show him some of my soccer trophies."

"Trophies?" Tsombé squealed.

"Little ones." He winked at Solange. "The kind a junior varsity benchwarmer would win."

Of course, Tsombé didn't understand all that, but he didn't have to. The bond growing between Tsombé Patchou and Paul didn't need much language.

By the time Solange returned with the inoculations drawn up, Tsombé was squealing with such strength she went running to make sure he wasn't in distress of some sort. But it wasn't distress she heard, much to her relief. It was delight. Paul was kneeling next to Tsombé, tossing the bean bag back and forth to him.

"He's got a pretty good pitching arm," Paul said, reaching into his pocket to pull out another piece of candy for the boy. "He might be a double threat."

"That means baseball and soccer," Tsombé explained in all earnestness.

"And are you going to show him your baseball trophies, too?" Solange asked, bending down next to the boy, getting ready to give him a shot.

"Little league. Pitcher. We went all the way to the international championships…" He drew in a long, dramatic breath. "Only to be beaten by the team from Japan. But we got…"

"I know. A tiny trophy."

"Actually, a pretty good-sized one. But I didn't get to keep it, so Tsombé will have to content himself with my personal trophies."

"Sixteen trophies," Tsombé interjected.

"Anything else?" Solange asked, as she gave the shots.

"Pinewood Derby trophies…"

"Little cars carved out of pine blocks," Tsombé explained. "You race them down a track."

"It looks like Tsombé's becoming quite the expert on your life, Paul."

Paul grinned.

It was a pity Paul didn't have children. That dozen he wanted would have suited him so nicely. "So you are going to take Tsombé back with you?"

He nodded. "First thing in the morning. Frère Léon is making the arrangements to help us get back to Ambrose, then he'll drive us the rest of the way in the truck. He'll talk to Tsombé's parents, too, and tell them how we're going to proceed with this."

Paul looked up at Solange, and she could see his lips curl into a smile even through the mask. "Doktè Candy would show you his trophies, too, if you'd like to come see them some time."

Without a word, Solange spun around and rushed back to the infirmary. "*Maman*," she whispered, as she opened the door. "Please, help me!" Once inside, she shut herself in the supply closet, turned off the light, slid to the floor, and wept.

CHAPTER EIGHT

SOLANGE slung her backpack down on her bed, then toppled down next to it. "Any word?" she asked Ayida. Tsombé had been on her mind all week. She knew Paul would take care of him, but that didn't stop her from worrying.

"The only thing was from Frère Léon, about Louise Babin, and he said to tell you the diagnosis was confirmed by the blood tests. Her X-rays show some orthopedic changes in her hands, but not much." She handed a sheet of paper to Solange. "This is what the people at that hospital gave Frère Léon to bring back to you."

Solange took a quick glance. Sed rate elevated, but not terribly. Same with the X-rays. Some damage, but not significant. A mild NSAID and exercise would do Louise just fine, and maybe keep the arthritis from advancing. Solange smiled, as she laid the paper aside. She always loved a good result, and this was a good result for Louise. "Nothing about Tsombé?"

Ayida shook her head. "Only that he's doing fine."

"In Miami," Frère Léon said from the doorway. "Paul took him over there a couple of days ago. He said the facility there for juveniles with TB will be able to manage Tsombé's case much better than he could because Tsombé's gone drug resistant."

"*Mon Dieu*," Solange whispered. That was a prognosis she certainly hadn't expected, and the little bit of joy she'd just taken from Louise Babin's diagnosis was wiped away. Tsombé had a difficult road ahead of him now. Apparently, he had become resistant to the normal drugs that were used to treat tuberculosis, which made him more prone to invasive infections.

"Paul said to tell you that he's *cautiously* optimistic about Tsombé's outcome." That meant he had hope, but he wasn't investing everything he had in that hope. Not yet, anyway. "Tsombé's responding favorably to initial treatment, and don't ask me what medicines he's being given because I couldn't tell you if you twisted my arm. And whose idea was it, anyway, to make the medical language so difficult?"

"But Paul said he's doing well?"

"Well enough that he's come back home. I don't think he would have left the boy there alone otherwise."

That was such a relief. In medicine, so many things were not under control, even with the most diligent of people working on them. Perhaps, for Tsombé, this would be brought under control quickly. She prayed that would be the case. "Has somebody talked to Tsombé's parents yet?"

Frère Léon shook his head. "Not yet. I just returned from Abbeville about an hour ago, and I thought I'd put my feet up and rest a little while before I hike over to tell them."

Solange let out a weary sigh. "It doesn't get any easier. I've got three more over on the east range with what I think is TB. I did the PPD test, and I'll go back over when it's time to read the results. I also gave everyone the BCG, and instructed the three people I think might have TB to wear masks and wash their hands frequently…a change of lifestyle they're going to hate. Paul has good luck in his instruction, though, so I'm keeping my fingers crossed I do, too." The PPD Solange referred to, purified protein derivative, was injected under the skin as a means of diagnosing TB. And the BCG, Bacille Calmette-Guerin, was a vaccine used as a TB preventative. "And I've got to get over to Tsombé's village and do the same as he's possibly exposed everyone there, so when you leave, let me know and I'll hike along with you."

Solange shoved her backpack to the floor and stretched out. "We don't have any patients in the infirmary, do we?" she asked Ayida.

"Just that no good Bobo Laventure. He's here to sleep it off again before he goes home to his wife. Just mixing with a devil of a hangover right now before he goes to face Mamirez." Ayida chuckled. "A devil of a wife."

Solange nodded. "Give him a couple of aspirin and wish him good luck with Mamirez."

"Can't blame her none for being angry like she gets," Ayida said. "She needs a *good* man."

"Don't we all," Solange said wistfully, as she closed her eyes.

"You could have one if you wanted him," Frère Léon called from the corridor outside Solange's room. His own room was just across from hers.

"Which I don't," Solange called back, then gestured for Ayida to shut her door. Only a week since she'd seen Paul and she missed him so badly it was turning into a physical ache. Absence made the heart grown fonder...she certainly knew what that meant. It did, in more ways than she'd counted on. The harder she'd tried not to think about Paul, the more she did.

* * *

"I've had a professional association with Solange just over a week now, and I'll admit that. But it has not affected my ability to run this hospital or to search out the means necessary to keep it going. In fact, I returned from Miami just this morning with some very promising leads to help me build a laboratory for all that equipment you've donated."

Bertrand Léandre gave Paul a tolerant smile, one that obviously had some other meaning to it. "She doesn't settle down, *mon ami*, and I'm worried that you might find yourself too caught up in her lifestyle. It's compelling, and a good cause, and I'm happy to support her. But I worry she will become a drain to you, and perhaps distract you in ways you shouldn't be distracted."

Paul nodded. Now he understood. Papa Léandre didn't want the two of them together. "So what's the bottom line here, Bertrand? Why don't you want me associating with your daughter?"

"Because you will not settle her. You will go one way, she will go another. And that doesn't work out."

"But it did with you, didn't it?"

"Absence, *mon ami*, is a very difficult thing to live with when you love someone desperately, as I did my Gabriella, and rarely have them at your side. It causes a man to do unspeakable things, things he despises himself for later. And I want better than that for my daughter. She deserves better than that, as my wife did."

Paul blinked back his surprise. The devoted Bertrand had been unfaithful to Gabriella, and he blamed their absences. He wasn't surprised, given Bertrand's larger-than-life lifestyle, but in a way he was taken aback just a little, because he'd truly believed Bertrand had adored Gabriella to the point of obsession. To adore, and yet to cheat? "I think you're reading much too much into my relationship with Solange," he said, already regretting what he'd just learned. Solange believed her parents had had a perfect marriage, and this would break her heart. Or frighten her about lasting relationships more than she already was. "We're well aware of the difficulties getting involved could cause, so we're not."

"It's never quite so simple, *mon ami*, and you're either naïve or foolish to think that it is, and I do not believe you to be a foolish man at all."

"You're forgetting that I was married once. That tends to take away the naïvety you seem to think I possess."

"Not so much as you might think. In a relationship, one often sees only what he, *or she*, wishes to see. My daughter and I have a strained relationship. She considers me domineering and I consider her willful, and I expect we both are all that, and more. But she wasted three years because she couldn't see, or she was seeing what she wished to see, and it took a great toll on her emotionally. She had to go away for a while to get over it. Another year gone by because of that and I'm not getting any younger."

"As in, you want to see her settled down into married life?"

"Married, settled and with an heir," he said quite frankly.

"You want a grandson," Paul stated.

"Gabriella gave me beautiful daughters, but not the son I needed. So now I have to wait for a grandson, and not one from you, to be perfectly blunt about it."

"Why?" Paul sputtered.

"I resisted Solaina's husband at first, because he didn't seem the type for Solaina. He has so many things to do in his life that I doubted he would ever settle down, which was what she needed. But I've found that he is the right man for her because he has settled her, and she's happy now. Not in the life I would have chosen, mind you, but she's made her choice and I've embraced her husband as my son because he *has* settled Solaina, and the prospects of my legacy are promising. But not you, *mon ami*. Solange needs someone to settle her, and that is not you, because you are not settled yourself. You are like me, always running off to pursue your business. Always leaving behind someone who cares for you. Was that not the case with the lovely Joanna?"

"I never cheated on Joanna. Not even in my heart. And if I were involved with Solange in anything other than a professional way, *which I'm not*, this is where the fight would start between us," Paul said, trying to keep his voice steady. How did Bertrand think he had the right to interfere in this, even if there really was nothing in which to interfere?

"But I am correct, and you recognize that. The temptations abound and you are a normal man. You may have resisted yesterday and you may resist today, but you cannot say what you will do tomorrow. I am the truest testament to that. And it would be a pity to dissolve our friendship because you cheated on my daughter. So the wiser course is to stay away from her so you don't find yourself in that position."

"Is that a threat?" Paul snapped.

"A wish. For my daughter. And even for you, although I'm sure you don't see it that way. I've lived the life you do, Paul. Always traveling, never with my wife, and it takes a toll. A horrible toll. More than anyone knows. I won't allow that for my daughter, even if it does mean threatening you. And, yes, even withdrawing my funds from your *hôpital* as a last resort."

This was incredible! Bertrand had just blindsided him because of Solange, or what he perceived to be some kind of relationship with Solange. "I'm not like you," Paul said. "If I were involved with Solange, or married to her, as you seem to think could become the case, I wouldn't cheat on her as you did on Gabriella. Is that what this is about? Your thinking I would do as you did?"

"Wouldn't you?" Bertrand asked, his composure suddenly so rigid, the chill of it was almost palpable.

"No, I would not!"

"I thought that once myself. Naïvety, I suppose. I was married to the perfect woman. And beautiful... If you think Solange is beautiful, and I'm sure you do, you should have seen her mother..." Bertrand shut his eyes and drew in a long, wistful breath, then let it out slowly. As he did, the icy feel in the room started to melt. "Naïvety, *mon ami*. A dreadful enemy, I'm afraid." He stood to leave. "I don't intend to cut off your donations, Paul. I thought we should talk this over first, see if we can come to some kind of an understanding on how to proceed from here, before your situation with my daughter escalates to a point where we cannot call it back."

"That sounds like a threat to me."

"I'd prefer to call it the over-protectiveness of a concerned father, and leave it at that. And someday, when you're a father yourself, you'll understand just what it is that I'm doing." He cast a knowing smile at Paul. "I'm sure you'll be seeing Solange before I will, so give her my best. Tell her there's a position opening up in a Stateside *hôpital* that might be of some interest to her. And I'd prefer that you keep this little chat between us. My daughters do not know the awful truth of my proclivities and it would torment them if they did." He laid his hand on the doorknob, then turned back. "She's a beautiful woman, Paul. I've known many beautiful women in my life and I understand these things. But in the interests of your *hôpital*, I would suggest that you stay focused on your work, and not on my daughter."

Behind his desk, Paul slumped down in his chair then rummaged through his desk drawer for an aspirin to take care of the pounding headache that was setting in. "Could have been worse," he muttered, shutting his eyes and rubbing at his temples after he took the pill. "Could have been a lot worse." He said the words, but he sure wasn't convinced by them.

Solange sat cross-legged in the grass under a giant banana tree, watching Frère Léon playing hacky sack with a few of the children from a neighboring village. It was a pleasant way to pass a few minutes, and she could almost envision Paul playing there, too. "I think you would like Paul very much, *maman*. He's a nice man. Kind. He takes good care of me, and doesn't let me get too stubborn, and you know how I can be stubborn. Unfortunately, that's the one quality I've inherited from *papa*." And one she didn't necessarily hate all the time, because quite often stubbornness suited her purposes. "Paul's so good with the children who come here, too, *maman*. Like their own *papas* would be, I think."

There were so many obstacles between them, but that was the insurmountable one. Children. He wanted them and she couldn't have them. Everything else could be worked out in a fashion, except that. And being barren was the great divide—the one that prevented the kiss, or the terms of endearment.

She missed Paul, though. Missed him desperately. "I fell in love so easily, *maman*. And so quickly." She'd been hoping for Paul's return almost from the moment he'd left, and had even made small adjustments to her schedule to allow her to be at The Mission more than she normally was just in case Paul did return, as he'd said he might. "Which is foolish, I know. But you cannot control what your heart does, can you? After all, you fell in love with *papa* and that was certainly never an easy life for you. So what should I do, *maman*?" The answer in her heart was *Paul*, and she smiled. "You aren't making this easy on me." *Paul* was not a practical answer to anything she needed, but such a nice one on which to dwell for a little while.

And her mother would have loved him.

In the background, Solange could hear the squeals of delight starting up from the children playing hacky sack. Paul was heading up the trail, she supposed. When he'd left with Tsombé, he'd said he might be back in just over a week, his schedule permitting. Now it was a week and three days, and here she was sitting with ridiculous butterflies in her stomach, all over the approach of a man who had no place in her future. It was all silliness, of course, like the actions of a schoolgirl with her first crush. She would get over it in due time. But this wasn't due time, she wasn't over it, and she caught herself wanting very much to turn around and watch him, maybe even run to him, as the children were doing.

Temptation wasn't the object, though, and even the simple act of thinking about Paul was more tempting than she cared to admit. So instead Solange leaned back against a tree, shut her eyes, and let the gentle tropical breeze sweep over her. Sometimes a few moments of nothing were wonderful, the balm to soothe everything. No commitments, no bother…a very cherished nothing because it rarely happened to her. She worked, she slept. End of story. That was her life. Drawing in a deep, cleansing breath, she let it out slowly as she relaxed into the moment...still anticipating Paul, however. He was the one thing that wouldn't be swept from her mind. "OK, *maman*," she whispered in desperation. "Here comes your answer, walking up the path. Now tell me what to do with him."

"Doktè Candy! Doktè Candy!" The cries of excitement from the children were almost unison.

"Toinette! Jean! Marie!" he called to them.

When had he learned their names? She wasn't even sure if *she* knew all the names of the children who scampered in from the villages. Suddenly, the gentle tropical breeze turned into a wash of melancholia. Of course he would remember their names, the way he loved children so. Her moment of nothing suddenly vanished, the old familiar lump of dread returned to the pit of her stomach, and she tensed up. "It's not going to work, *maman*. It's simply not going to work."

Paul waved briefly at her, but his attention was solely for the children as he tossed candy and fruit to them. And balls this time, instead of the hacky sacks. "He's an amazing man," Frère Léon said, sitting himself down next to Solange and handing her an apple as he adjusted his robe to cover his ankles. "The way he gets about, the way he gets things done..."

"It's not working," Solange said, wiping her apple on the leg of her shorts. "He may have the most amazing attributes of any man in the world, but I've sworn off men, and you're not going to convince me to do otherwise."

"You'll change your mind."

"Not a chance."

"So you're hating the male gender today?"

"I'm not particularly fond of what several members of that

gender have done to me and to people I love but, no, I don't hate the gender as a whole."

"You've grown wiser since Mauricio. That whole ugly situation may not have turned out as you probably thought it would the first time you met him, but look what you've done since then. Look what you've done with your life, and to the lives of the people around you. I'd say that in spite of not being particularly fond of his actions, and they were abominable, you've managed much better without him."

"I had to. There wasn't another choice."

"Which is why I said you'll change your mind. Because you will. We evolve, Solange. Evolve, or die."

"Don't hold your breath on my evolution. I've climbed out of the primordial ooze and I'm happy right where I am, thank you very much."

Frère Léon chuckled. "You always were such a stubborn one."

"Are you OK, Solange?" Paul asked, sitting down on the other side of her, now that the children had scurried away home with their new toys. "You look tired."

"Because she doesn't sleep." Frère Léon supplied. "An hour here, an hour there, but never enough to stay rested. We were all concerned about that when she came to stay with us..." He caught himself about to divulge something he shouldn't, and took a bite of apple instead of continuing or backtracking.

"Your father mentioned that you went away for some rest. Was it to Frère Léon's cloister?"

"Actually, it's a monastery," Frère Léon said. "Or I suppose you could call it a habitat of monks. I think abode is nice, though—"

"My father was discussing me?" Solange interrupted.

"His concerns for you," Paul said.

"Which are?"

"Your lifestyle, basically. He seems to be against it."

"Of course he's against it," Solange snapped. "He didn't choose it."

"Speaking of which, he did mention that there's an opening in one of the hospitals Stateside. Are you looking for another position?"

"Monsieur Léandre is always looking out on behalf of his daughter," Frère Léon said. "He believes that it's not fitting that she should be running around in the mountains with an old man such as myself, who wears long robes and sandals." He pulled back his robe to reveal his feet and wiggle his toes. "There's nothing wrong with my sandals," he added. "Perfectly good footwear, and that's what I said to Monsieur when he told me that Solange needed better." He smiled. "So now the man believes me to be daft as well as poorly dressed."

"What else did he say," Solange butt in impatiently, "about my going away for that rest?" Surely her father didn't know. She hadn't told him about her hysterectomy, and she wasn't going to. It didn't matter, of course, if he did know. But there were things in her life she wanted to keep private. At least for now, when the wound hadn't yet healed in an emotional sense.

"That after you left Mauricio it took you a while to get over it. And I know how that feels. Even though Joanna and I were quite friendly about our parting, there was that initial sense of loss. A nice retreat might have done me some good." He glanced over Frère Léon, faking a scowl. "You never offered to take me in."

"Because you can't stay in the same place for more than a day or two. We would have had to tie you down to keep you there, then you would have gone insane, and what would we have done with you then?"

Solange shut her eyes and listened to the banter of the two men. She didn't believe her father knew about her hysterectomy, or Paul, for that matter, and she was relieved. It had been such a rocky time in her life...sick on and off for two years. And enduring Mauricio's reactions over it.

Now she fought the daily hormone skirmish...not enough, too much. High, low. Grumpy. And all slamming in in what seemed to be the same blink of an eye,

She'd had endometriosis. The lining of the uterus, the endometrium, had gone haywire on her. The cells and tissues normally lining the uterus had been growing outside it, causing her all sorts of havoc—pain, gastro-intestinal problems, urinary difficulties, lots of bleeding, terrible menstrual cramps. She had also been diagnosed with a tumor, and she shuddered, thinking about that horribly long wait to find out if it had been cancerous. Luckily, it hadn't been. It was called, in layman's terms, a chocolate cyst. But as Allain might have said, it had been quacking like a low-grade cancer. That had been the last straw. Two years of hell, and she'd decided to end it. Have it all removed. Be done with it.

Mauricio had been marginally supportive until he'd realized that she had been becoming scant in the womanly duty department. Then her battle with endometriosis had been an inconvenience to him. *To him!* But like an idiot, she'd clung to him, probably because there had been no one else to cling to at the time. Of course, the day she'd told him her decision to have the surgery had been a classic. "Will you grow facial hair?" he'd asked. That had been his concern—facial hair!

Now it seemed almost funny, but at the time it had been

devastating. By the next day, she'd left him. Her illness, along with his moving-on-up attitude... She just hadn't wanted to be bothered with a man who had been more concerned with the possibility of facial hair than the fact that she was going to have a major, life-altering surgery. She chuckled aloud, thinking about it.

"I didn't think it was funny," Paul said.

"What?" Solange said, homing back into the conversation.

"That Joanna had completely left me for almost a week before I noticed. Frère Léon was just pointing out another of my horrible shortfalls as a husband."

"I wasn't laughing at that," Solange said. "I'd just thought of a bearded lady I saw in the circus once."

"On that bizarre note, I think I'll leave you two and go scrounge a snack for myself. The apple was delicious, but not nearly enough." Frère Léon patted his belly. "Not *nearly* enough." He stood, straightened his robe, then bounced off in the direction of the kitchen.

"Was it a breakdown?" Paul asked, rather quickly.

"What? My going to stay with the monks?"

"Your father is over-protective, and I just thought that it might have been because—"

"Yes," Solange interrupted. "It was a breakdown. Not in the sense that I was bouncing off the walls or doing crazy things. But I did withdraw a bit. I needed time alone, to reflect, to figure out what I was going to do next in my life. Mauricio was moving into a life I didn't want, and one, ultimately, he didn't want me in, and that's all there was to it. Frère Léon took me in."

"I'm so sorry," he whispered, taking her hand.

She didn't refuse him. She should have, but his touch felt

so good, and she craved it like she'd never craved anything before. "It wasn't a tragedy, Paul. There's nothing to be sorry about. I went, I rested, I left. It was merely a time in my life when I was vulnerable to things I shouldn't have been, so I shut myself away until I was better. No psychotropic drugs, no counseling, no shock therapy. Just reflection."

"And the reflection led you here?"

"With the aid of Frère Léon, yes, it did. I needed a fresh start, and it was right here, waiting for me when I was ready." All these words to him were the truth. The part of her story he was entitled to know.

"Why don't you take the rest of the day off, Solange. Sleep, eat some of the fruit I brought." He slipped a bar of lavender-scented soap from his pocket and handed it to her. "Pamper yourself a little."

She raised the soap to her nose, savoring the scent of it for a moment through the mask. Such a small thing, a bar of soap. But he couldn't have brought her anything she would appreciate more. "Thank you," she said.

"I would have brought chocolates and champagne, but I remember what happened to the last man who brought them to you." Her gave a fake shudder. "I didn't hike all the way here for that. Also, I brought you these." He handed a sample packet of medicine to her. Pyroxicam. A drug used for rheumatoid arthritis. "Maybe Louise Babin will tolerate this well. It was lying around in my sample drawer, and I thought that..." He shrugged. "I thought that I might use it as a good excuse to come see you."

"The soap is wonderful. And so is the pyroxicam." So was having him here, no matter the reason. "Thank you for everything."

"So go pamper yourself for an hour or two, Solange," he said. "I'll take over your duties here."

"The only person in the infirmary is Bobo Laventure, and I don't think he exactly needs help, unless you have some aspirin handy for his hangover."

"When do you go out again?"

"Day after tomorrow. Keskeya and Ayida are taking the day off tomorrow to go to Abbeville for some shopping. I'll stay here just in case anybody comes along. I need to get some things arranged in the infirmary, anyway. Another shipment of medical goods came in and I haven't had time to store them properly. I also have some medical journals I'd like to catch up on. Maybe go take a splash in the falls, if I have enough time."

"Did I ever mention that I have a small collection of swimming trophies? That I'm very good in the water?"

"Is that a hint that you want to stay on, Doctor?"

"It could be. No strings attached, of course."

"No strings," she confirmed.

"Promise."

She looked into his eyes, those gorgeous blue eyes, and somehow she didn't believe that promise. Somehow, she didn't want to.

CHAPTER NINE

"'CONSISTENT with *empyema necessitatis*. Although the outcome of the pleural biopsy was culture-negative, the pleural-fluid culture was positive for *Mycobacterium tuberculosis*. Since the mycobacteria were, in full, susceptible to all antimycobacterial agents, the patient began therapy with a standard antituberculosis regimen, and his condition improved.' Whew!" Paul took in a deep breath, laughed, and flung the medical journal out into the grass. "I could have told them that!" he exclaimed, lying down on the blanket next to Solange, so they were both now gazing up at the sky. With a discreet picnic hamper separating them, of course. He'd watched Solange place it just so an hour ago, the intention of that little action quite obvious. That was the line. Their relationship stopped at the loaf of crusty bread.

"You could have told them that in plain English, no less." Solange added. "They took an X-ray, discovered the condition, and treated it. I'll bet the person writing that article was being paid by the word." She laughed. "I skipped the jargon class in medical school. Preferred poetry and literature. *Good* literature."

"I think the philosophy is that they can't make it sound too simple or us poor slobs might make it out of medical school in three years instead of four."

"I did make it out in three," Solange replied. "Would have been less, but I was taking a pottery class at the university at the same time, so I wasn't in any hurry to go. And besides, I rather liked medical school. It was simple then. You worked twenty hours a day, somebody yelled at you because you didn't get it right, and somebody yelled at them because *they* didn't get it right. It's a pretty standard order, I think, that goes on the same way until they give you a diploma and turn you loose on an unsuspecting public."

Paul was tempted to raise up and gaze over the hamper at her for a bit, but instead he stayed safe behind it. It was a perfect day for this little impromptu picnic: reading a medical journal on a blanket in the grass; sipping fresh fruit juice from tumblers; eating crusty bread and hard cheese. Turning this day into a short holiday hadn't been his intention when the day had started, but now he was glad it had turned out this way. It was a respite he desperately needed in an otherwise back-breaking schedule, and it was nice to lie here with his pants rolled up to his knees, barefooted, and count the clouds. *With Solange.* That was the best part. There were moments to savor because he didn't know how many more he'd be allowed. "In three years? You finished medical school in three years? Are you trying to show me up?" He chuckled. "Because if you are, you succeeded brilliantly, Doctor."

"If it took you more than three years, Doctor, I suppose I did." Laughing, Solange raised up to pluck two coconut cookies from the hamper, the chocolate-dipped macaroons a Chef Frère Léon specialty, and tossed one over to Paul. Then she lay back down.

"It seemed like it took a dozen years, but it was a mere four. And it wasn't so bad later, during my residency, once I got to the top of the yelling heap. But that was sure one hard climb."

"You made chief resident?" she asked.

"Yep. There *was* a time when I was ambitious like that. I thought it would look good on my résumé and snag me that job to which I was aspiring. Then I'd buy an awesome set of golf clubs, one like the pros would assemble—my three-wood a Callaway S2H2, my irons Maxfli Revolution, my putter—"

"Whoa," Solange interrupted, waving at Paul over the top of the hamper. "At least I understood the medical jargon, but now you're talking in a completely foreign language."

"A Ping Anser 2," he persisted. "I need just a moment to savor the fantasy because until you've had one of those babies in your hands you don't know what it's like to putt."

"Lesson learned," she giggled. "Never come between a man and his fantasy putter."

"His Ping Anser 2."

"Am I sensing a little wistfulness for the good old days?"

"No. But I still like a good round of golf when I can get to it. Just not on the clubs I once thought I would own."

"Well, putters and drivers aside, being chief resident does look good on your résumé, even out here. And I'm impressed."

Paul chuckled. "Out here, what's even more impressive is knowing the correct bug repellent and sunscreen SPF factor."

"Then I take it you're not waxing melancholy over your schooldays?"

"Hell, no. I had other things to do, and all I wanted was to get out and into the real world. Which was what I got, because this is just about as real as it comes." He popped the cookie into his mouth, rose to fish another out of the hamper, and became distracted watching Solange eat her cookie. It was a methodical process, one little nibble at a time. When she caught him watching her, she smiled shyly and waved off the next cookie he was holding out to her. "I'll bet you don't even spill crumbs," he said.

"I thought we were talking about golf."

"Actually, I was talking about golf, and probably boring you to death. So enough about me. Tell me about you, Solange. Golfing was always at the top of my leisure-hours list. What's at the top of yours?"

"I told you I'd taken pottery classes… I love it, really. It may not be as exciting as owning a Ping Anser 2, but someday I'd like to have my own little studio and makes plates and bowls or something. Maybe sell them to the tourists."

Paul pushed the hamper out of the way, then reached over and took Solange's hand into his own. "That's a beautiful hand with which to throw pots," he said. "Delicate. Soft. You would have a nice feel for the clay." Impulsively, he kissed her hand, then he laid it back at her side and pulled the hamper back between them. "And I'll buy the first one out of the kiln. So, now that we've eaten, read those stimulating medical articles and spilled all our secret hopes and dreams, I seem to recall something about a waterfall?"

"Would you like to go for a swim?" Solange asked, sitting up.

"With, or without clothes?"

She studied his face for a moment—the laughter in his eyes, the crinkling of a smile around his mouth. It was so comfortable here with him, more comfortable than she'd ever been with anybody except, perhaps, her mother. And she didn't want this day to ever end. "No subtleties in that suggestion, are there?"

"Subtleties are required?" He arched suggestive eyebrows at her.

"No, but skivvies are required," she said.

"And what if I don't wear skivvies?"

Solange tossed him an audacious smile. "I *am* a doctor after all. I'd be professional about it. *Totally* professional."

"Damn," he muttered, standing. "Just when I was hoping for something unprofessional."

"Not me, Doctor. My waterfall, my rules."

It had been weeks since she'd been there and as she stepped off the trail over to the small lake and gazed across it to the waterfall on the opposite side, she realized what a perfect place this would be for a home. She would be standing at the picture window right now, enamored all over again with the backdrop of the cliffs and the little cascade of water spilling over them into the lake below. She would be falling in love afresh with the palisade of lush green tropical trees, with the ground cover of tropical flowers in swathes of oranges and reds and pinks.

This little patch of heaven, which she'd inherited from her mother, was such an unblemished paradise. They'd picnicked and played under the falls here, and made necklaces of the flowers. And they'd talked about the little cottage her mother would build here someday. Just *their* little secret.

To Solange, this was Kijé in its fullest splendor. Her special place. And it was where she was closest to her mother. She'd brought no one here before—not her sister or father, not Ayida or Keskeya, not even Frère Léon. Paul was the first...the first in many ways.

Without saying a word to Paul, Solange waded into the lake

until she was up to her knees. "It doesn't get much deeper than this, city boy," she called back to him. "No gators, no piranhas, so what are you waiting for?"

Shrugging, Paul kicked off his shoes, then unbuttoned his cotton shirt and tossed it aside. She'd seen his bare chest before, but a glance still caused her breath to catch in her throat, and she turned away quickly, trying to ignore the feeling that this was a mistake. A total mistake that could have disastrous results.

"One day," she whispered, watching Paul standing on the shore of the lake, rolling his pants up another couple of hitches until they were just above his knees. "He is magnificent, *maman*. Beautiful in a way I never thought a man could be." Too bad he hadn't stripped off completely, but it was probably for the best. Especially as, in turn, he might expect the same from her, and that's something she would never do. Not in broad daylight. She could barely look at that scar herself—the ugly reminder of an ugly time—and she would *never* let him see it. "Last one to the falls forfeits his swimming trophies," she called, laughing.

"You're assuming that I'll lose," he yelled, wading out to the point where he could actually swim. By the time those words were out, Solange was breast-stroking her way across the lake, feeling nothing but the warm water sloshing over her body and hearing nothing but her own breathing. She needed this. With, or without, Paul, she truly needed this. Although, admittedly, it was much better with him.

As Solange dragged herself up on the distant shore—the outcropping of rocks next to the falls—Paul stepped out from under the cascade, grinning at her. "How did you do that?" she squealed, pushing her hair back from her face.

"Quite handily, actually. So, do *you* have any swimming trophies that I get to claim as my prize?"

"Obviously not." The tan cotton of his trousers was clinging to him like a second skin and it was quite apparent to her that he wore no skivvies underneath. Immediately, she dropped her eyes to the ground, then fought with herself about taking a quick peek. When he wasn't looking, of course. But he was looking at her...*staring*, more like it. She could feel the burn of his eyes on her, raking her from head to toe, without even looking at him. "The only trophy I received was for chess, but I'll make sure you have it."

"Chess?"

She braved a brief look then cast her eyes downward again. "And what's wrong with chess?"

"Nothing's *wrong* with chess. But I would taken you for an athlete." He held out his hand. "Care to join me under here? We did come to splash about in the falls, didn't we?"

"I played a bit of tennis," she said, taking a few steps closer.

"You'd look stunning in tennis whites," he commented, his hand still outstretched. "Your opponent wouldn't stand a chance, if it was a man. He'd be dazzled..."

"I never won a trophy," she said.

"Playing on the same court with you would be the trophy."

She reached out and took his hand, but hesitated to go any closer. "We shouldn't," she whispered shyly.

"Life is full of shouldn'ts, Solange. And there are so few shoulds."

"Paul, I just—" she started to protest, but he raised his finger to her lips.

"Shh," he whispered. "Do this with your heart, Solange. Not with your head."

Her heart. It was so full of Paul it felt it would burst. It's what she wanted, of course. No *shouldn't* about this. It's all she wanted, and her heart wouldn't refuse. "Just today," she whispered. "Just this one day…"

Finally, she braved a full look, but only at his face. His beautiful face. This was the man she loved. The only man she had ever loved. And she had no will to resist him.

Before Solange had another chance to talk herself out of it, she was wrapped in his arms, and the feel of him pressed tightly to her exploded into a million twinkling lights through her senses, the force of it like nothing she'd ever before known. The soft mat of his wet chest hair on her cheek, the feel of his arousal through the thin cotton of his trousers…there was no turning back from this now, not that she could. Not that she would.

"Are you sure?" he whispered. His voice so tender and full of concern it brought tears to her eyes…tears for the way he cared, and tears because after this, it couldn't be again.

"Yes, I'm sure."

The words were barely out before he pressed his lips to hers, parting them with his tongue. He tasted exotic, she thought. Champagne and mango. And as his soft hands sought her body, stroking her thighs first, then wiggling up under her shorts to find that she, like he, wore no skivvies, she strained to push herself even closer to him, to feel more of his tongue, more of his hand.

Too eager, she thought as she slid her hands around his neck. Too eager, far too inexperienced for all her experience… Too wanting of it all right now.

His hand moved upward, seeking her breast, and when he found her nipple he taunted it into a peak. "Paul," she moaned, as he paused long enough to pull her buttoned shirt right over her head.

"So beautiful," he said, stepping back to feast his eyes.

He reached out to stroke her breasts. First the left, then the right, and she sucked in a deep breath and held it, finally glancing down at the wet and oh, so deliciously see-through fabric of his trousers.

"Shall I take them off you?" she asked, almost shyly.

"Like I've never wanted anything taken off me in my entire life." His voice was rough and so full of need, her own need suddenly rose to a point she'd never before known, and it surprised and delighted her because she'd feared she would never have these kinds of feelings flow through her.

Without a word, Solange stepped forward and ran her fingers lightly over his pectorals. Nice, hard…muscles worthy of an athletic trophy. Then she moved on down the ridges of his ribs and across his rippling abdomen. When she reached the beltline of his trousers, he sucked in a sharp breath and held it as she unfastened the single button, inching the zipper slowly down.

Her fingers brushed over his arousal as the zipper parted, causing him to hiss out his first breath and gasp in another. "I did admire you that first night at my father's party," she whispered, as she peeled his wet, clingy pants down over his hips. "Maybe not to this extent, but I thought about having you in the raspberry bubble bath with me."

"Had you asked…"

Solange laughed, bending to grab his slacks and toss them out of the way. "Had you stayed…"

"You're killing me, saying something like that. Do you know how much I wanted to stay?"

She glanced up at him, her eyes raking leisurely over him, *all* of him, as they trailed up to his face. "As much as you do now?"

Paul reached for Solange, pulling her up to him, to his full measure, then he pushed the hair away from her neck and planted a row of quick, red-hot kisses there. "Need help with your shorts?" he growled. "I've got some sexy possibilities on how to get them off you."

Remove her shorts! Oh, no! She was so close to that, but she couldn't. Not like this. "In the water," she gasped, trying to fight back the momentary panic trying to rise up and ruin everything. "Under the falls."

"Sounds good to me," he breathed, grabbing her by the hand and pulling her through the water until they were nearly waist deep, and situated directly below the cataract. "You're so beautiful," he said, cupping his hand around the sleek curve of her breast, then bending to kiss it. "And I've wanted to do *this* since that first night." He brushed his thumb over the crown of her nipple, then again and again, each stroke causing her to breathe harder and deeper, each stroke sending delectable jolts of electricity and arousal out to the very last nerve ending in the tips of her fingers and toes. And just when she thought she would explode, he pressed both her breasts together and kissed first one, then the other, then caught the sepia tip of her left nipple in his mouth and nibbled lightly.

Solange trembled with delight, wanting much more of it, and when Paul took her hand to draw her over to a round granite boulder sunken halfway into the water, then leaned her back against it, she didn't protest when he reached under the water's surface to pull off her shorts and pleasure her in ways she'd never known. Instantly, she was aching with the sheer, raw need of wanting him, thrusting herself at him when he stopped for a second to toss her shorts up onto the rock. When he reached around to cup her bottom in his hands and pull her hard against him, she gasped from the feel of his desire. "Paul," she choked, reaching down into the water to pleasure him as he had done her.

"You don't know how much this pains me," he choked, "but I'm not..."

She looked up at him, her eyes wide and innocent. "Not what?" she whispered, curling her mouth into a sexy smile. "Because from what I'm feeling, you definitely are."

Stupid! To come out here with her, wanting this like he did, and not be prepared for it. Even more stupid to coax her out then tell her he couldn't finish. But he had to. "Not prepared," he groaned. "No..."

He heard a small gasp slip through her lips, then saw a look of hesitation shadow her eyes. But only for a moment. "I am," she said, the sexy smile returning to her lips.

"Are you sure?"

She nodded. And that's all it took. Paul pulled her back to him, and kissed her hard. She tasted like sex, like a pure, sweet ambrosia he'd never tasted before, and as much as he wanted to indulge in so many more pleasures to be found in her, it wasn't to be. The urgency of his need was crashing at him so hard it was nearly painful. And the sweet inebriation of having the most beautiful woman in the world here in his arms like this was driving him to a place he'd never before known. As he pressed himself to her, the water lazily licking their bodies up to their waists, he so desperately wanted to say the words imploring to be let out, but he wouldn't, for fear she would take flight like a bird to some far-off branch, and he would never again get her back.

But as he joined with her, the words exploded in his brain, over and over, beating at him as no emotion ever had. *I love you, Solange!*

Dear God, he did, like he'd never known could be possible.

"Cheese?" Solange asked, cutting off a wedge for herself. She was famished, all afterglow and starving. And nervous, of course. How to react to him now? That was a huge question and an even huger concern, because she didn't want to throw away the friendship with him. It was too precious to toss aside, and now her head had overtaken her heart, and the logic of the moment dictated that they shouldn't have done what they had, that friendships never survived after something like that had happened, because once you'd gone forward, you could never go back.

And she desperately wanted him for a friend, even though she couldn't have him as a lover. So, yes, she was definitely feeling the afterglow, but she was also feeling apprehension. Besides that, what were you supposed to do after you put your clothes back on? Sit and chat? Smoke a cigarette, even though she didn't smoke? Mauricio had always turned over and gone to sleep straight away, while she'd stayed awake, staring at the ceiling, sometimes for hours, trying to figure out why the longing was still there. Right now, though, Paul was definitely not sleeping, and she definitely didn't have any leftover longings.

Paul grinned over at her lazily, and reached for the slice she was handing to him. "So, I thought maybe we'd read another article in the medical journal now, before we lose the light."

After they'd made love, they'd splashed around in the water like children for a while, then had swum back to their blanket. She wasn't yet dry, neither was he, and it was all she could do to keep her eyes off him as he'd yet to put his shirt back on. But one long look, and she knew she would start it again. There was no will left in her. And she so desperately needed that will—that resolve—back, because her one day was almost at an end now. The sun would be setting shortly, and it would be over. Which was the way it was meant to be.

"How about you read that article, *to yourself*, while I sit here and watch the sunset?"

"May I share the sunset with you?" he asked, reaching over to take her hand. The hamper no longer separated them on the blanket. Nothing did.

"I'd love for you to share it with me," she whispered, scooting over closer to him. As she did, he sat up and pulled her into his arms, and they stayed that way, clinging together, breathing as one, *being as one*, until the night skies overtook the end of the day. "We have to go back," Solange finally whispered, regretting that she had to break the perfect mood.

"In a little while," he said, as he unbuttoned her blouse. "You had your day, and now it's my night."

She wasn't sure how long it had been raining when she opened her eyes, but it was still dark and the blanket in which they were wrapped was soaked all the way through. She was nestled tight into Paul, though, and the chill of the dampness had not yet set in.

In the near distance she could hear the sound of the rain beating down on the trees. It was a hypnotic sound, its methodical rhythm lulling her, and Solange gave thought to staying there with Paul, as they were, in the rain. But common sense prevailed. She had clinic in the morning, then later she intended to set out for one of the villages a good three-hour hike from The Mission and spend the night there so she could start fresh the following morning.

All of this meant she had to get back home, sleep if there was any time left, and start the morning like she should—bright, alert and ready to face whatever the day brought.

"Paul," she said, nudging him. "We've got to get back." She pulled back the soggy picnic blanket and started to emerge from the cocoon they'd made around themselves.

"Another ten minutes," he moaned.

"So you're one of those…always wanting ten minutes more, then another ten, then another ten." She yanked the blanket all the way off him, then leaned over and smacked him playfully on his bare bottom. "Won't work, Doctor."

"Don't know the way back in the dark," he protested.

"I do."

"You're not going to be talked out of this, are you?" He sat up and stretched, then rubbed the rain from his eyes. "And I was in the middle of such a nice dream." He grabbed Solange by the hand, pulled her over to him and placed a kiss on her forehead. "There was this gorgeous jungle doctor who was witching me…"

Solange pulled away, laughing. "Like it or not, we've got to leave here, city boy, and stalling won't do you any good. As soon as I've gathered our picnic things, I'm hiking back down the trail."

"With or without me?" Paul asked, reaching for his shirt, even though it was soaked.

"Want your pants, too?" she asked, holding them out for him.

"What I want is more than one day and one night, Solange.

I want to be more than friends. And before you stop me, I've been giving this a lot of thought. It might not be a traditional arrangement, with me going one way and you going another, but neither of us have the expectation that we can, or even want, to hold the other one back. So we might not get quantity hours together, but we can make up for that in quality. And I'm convinced of it. My turnaround, Solange. You are my turnaround, and I can be yours if you'll let me."

"No," she choked. "That's not what this is about, Paul. Not getting involved in something more than what we have."

"Isn't it? I'm not going to be traveling for ever, Solange. In another two or three years I hope to have the hospital solid financially so I don't have to go out looking for money nearly as much. And then we can work on a real life, you doing what you do and me…well, maybe being a doctor at the hospital again, and if we're lucky, I'll stay behind to raise a few children while their mother is doing marvelous things in the mountain villages. We'll work that out when the time comes. And I know this sounds like an incredible way to live, but we can do it, Solange. It wasn't meant to be in my first marriage because that relationship wasn't meant to be. I've spent a lot of time telling myself it was the lifestyle that broke up Joanna and me when it was always the two people involved in the lifestyle. But for us…we know how we have to live, and we would be going into it knowing what it was about. The highs, the lows, the absences…"

Paul drew in a quick breath and continued. "It wasn't what I wanted, and definitely not what I expected at this place in my life. But now it's all I can think about. The two of us, working it out together, whatever that turns out to be."

Solange shut her eyes and concentrated on the rain falling

down on her. This is what she had feared most, and now it had happened. And it couldn't be undone. "I can't, Paul. You've known that all along, that I won't be involved. Not with you, not with anybody. It was a wonderful day, but it's over."

Her tears mixed with the rain now. The bitter with the sweet. "I'm sorry, but I can't." Now it was over between them. All of it.

CHAPTER TEN

"I HEARD there's a storm coming in this evening or tomorrow. I want to be back at the infirmary before it hits," Solange told Ayida. Frère Léon was off to one of the villages and somebody had to go into Abbeville to pick up the lab results for Hennrick Vareaux. Solange suspected an underactive thyroid, and she needed the final confirmation before she put him on a course of drugs. For the past three weeks Frère Léon had run the errands to Abbeville, and more specifically to Paul's hospital, but today that wasn't going to be the case. No one was in the infirmary and she had no appointments out in the villages until the day after tomorrow, so the rest of the afternoon was to be spent going to a place she'd tried not thinking about for the past twenty-one days.

A quick trip down, a quick trip back. If Paul did happen to be there, she would be cordial. *How are you, Doctor? How is your fundraising going?* That would be sufficient, especially as he had made no move to return to The Mission since that night she'd rejected him. Of course, she didn't blame him for that. How could she when he'd given her his heart and she'd thrown it right back at him?

"And you're going to take some time for that handsome man of yours?" Ayida asked.

"He's not my man," Solange snapped.

"Then why do you get so grumpy when we mention him? And sometimes I see you staring off at the mountain, and from the moony look on your face you're certainly not thinking about medicine."

"I get grumpy because you bring up the subject of Dr Killian at least ten times a day, and I'm tired of it. That's why!"

"If you'd get over yourself and go after him to tell him you're sorry for sending him away like you did, I wouldn't have to keep talking about him." She chuckled good-naturedly in spite of Solange's sour mood. "It makes no good sense to me, putting him off like you do when it's as plain as Frère Léon's bald head that you're in love with the man. And in these parts we all know that only the fool turns his, *or her*, back on love. I wouldn't have got myself six kiddies of my own if I had."

Solange cast her an angry look. "Well, we all know I won't be having six kiddies, don't we?"

"If the womanly thing is such a bother, fix it."

"Why didn't I think of that? I'll just call my doctor and ask him to put my ovaries back in."

Ayida sat down on the bench next to Solange and put her arms around Solange's shoulders. On the other side of the compound, Keskeya was instructing a few children in the fine art of the hacky sack. Even when Paul wasn't here, his presence was, in so many ways. Louise Babin was having amazing results with her arthritis treatment and weaving baskets galore now. The news on Tsombé Patchou was encouraging, too. In another few weeks he would return here to the infirmary for observation, then a few weeks after that he'd go home.

Yes, Paul was everywhere, and every time she saw his influence, the wound opened even more. "I'm sorry," she said to Ayida. "It's not easy."

Ayida sniffed impatiently. "It's not easy because you're keeping your womanly thing from that man!" She gave her head a sharp, exasperated shake. "That's what you're doing, isn't it? Hiding it from him?"

"Because my *womanly thing* is none of that man's business." She couldn't do this, not now, so Solange patted Ayida on the arm, then squirmed out of her hold. "I'll be back by dark. Tell Frère Léon, when he returns, that I'll be starting clinic a little earlier than usual tomorrow, and if he doesn't have other plans I'd like for him to hike to the villages with me for the next couple of days."

"I know you don't want my opinion, but I'll give it to you anyway because I'm old enough I can do that and get away with it." She twisted to look Solange directly in the eye. "This is no good, what you're doing. You're wasting time that you'll never get back. When I think of all the time I wasted with my man Souie…" She paused to brush away a tear starting to slide down her cheek. "They're gone from you all too soon, and after that is when you'll be regretting even more that you didn't have all the time with them that you could have had. I had thirty good years with Souie and if I had the chance for one more minute, I wouldn't be sitting here all grumpy over something that can't be helped, like you're doing." The tone of her voice went soft, and a yearning smile crossed her face. "I've got no more chances with my man, but you've still got a chance with yours."

"That chance passed me by," Solange said, bending forward to kiss Ayida's cheek.

Paul stepped outside onto the porch for no other reason than he felt trapped inside the hospital today. In fact, for the past three weeks, every time he returned here, that feeling of claustrophobia set in. It wasn't the walls that confined him, though. It was his thoughts. And Solange's rejection. The more he thought about it the angrier he got, and being away from Kijé helped during the hours when he had enough to do to occupy his mind. But in those lean minutes when he allowed his thoughts to wander, that's when it hit him again—that verbal slam to the gut that nearly doubled him over.

And now, being back home, it was all spinning around him one more time. Deep down, he knew Solange had feelings for him. He wasn't so blinded by his own feelings for her that he'd lost all objectivity. She did care for him, and she was the kind of woman who didn't step lightly into a relationship. That was something Paul trusted with all his heart. But, damn it, he certainly hadn't expected a total rejection from her. Maybe a put-off, or a promise for something later, or even a casual commitment to meet whenever they could. Any of those would have been fine, even though at the time, stupidly enough, he'd been thinking something more permanent. Like marriage.

Yes, that was stupid. But her reaction...

He wasn't over it. Didn't know how he could be. Not when there were so many reminders of her...the *tap-taps*, the fragrances, the whole damned island!

Paul glanced at his watch. Frère Léon would be there shortly to pick up the lab results. He'd been very good keeping Paul informed about Solange. Not that it mattered. But, still, he had to know. Just because she'd flatly rejected him, that didn't mean that he'd flatly fallen out of love. And he looked forward to the little tidbits of information Frère Léon always brought him. It was probably just a pathetic effort that, in the end, would get him nowhere. But right now it still connected him to her, and he needed that connection very badly.

Right now, though, right at this very moment he was as angry as hell at himself for being angry as hell at Solange. So maybe this distance was good. Because he needed to be away from her and have a good, rational think about the whole exasperating situation. If he was lucky, he would put it into its proper perspective, if that was at all possible now, given his feelings for her. Then in another week, when he returned from his next business trip to Boston, maybe he wouldn't be in such a state. And the week after that…

"We need to talk," Solange said, stepping into Paul's office. She hadn't wanted to see him, but what Ayida had said… Paul deserved an explanation. He was making plans for a future with a woman who couldn't give him what he wanted. As much as that was a private matter, she'd thought about it for the entire drive into Abbeville and had decided that he had to know. It was only fair. Then he could get over it and find another way.

But now, seeing the deep scowl set into his brow, and the fact that there was no longer a twinkle in his eyes… "You look tired," she said softly.

"Would you care?" he snapped, not bothering to get up from his chair.

"Of course I care, Paul. But that's not the point."

"But it is. That's always been the point, Solange. What *you* care about. And I was a fool because you made that pretty clear right from the start, and like an idiot I went and fell in love with you anyway because I thought…" He drew in a sharp breath, expelled it in a huff, and shook his head. "It doesn't matter what I thought. You did what you told me you would do, and I should have listened to you in the first place when you said that you wouldn't get involved."

"But I didn't tell you everything," Solange cried.

"You told me enough," he said, spinning his chair to face the window. "You warned me away from you, then your father warned me away from you, and, like an idiot, I didn't take the hint. Not from either of you."

"My father?"

"None other… He said that I'm not settled enough, and that you need someone who's settled. But he's wrong, isn't he? You're afraid of being settled. You're afraid that I *will* settle you."

"Paul, I didn't know he'd said something to you!"

"That's who he is and what he does, Solange, and I can deal with it. But it really doesn't matter now, does it? Apparently it takes a hurricane to hit me over the head, because I really did believe that we'd work it out in spite of our fears, our jobs, our pasts, your father… But we won't, Solange. You won't let us."

She didn't blame him for being angry. Perhaps it was for the best, at least as far as Paul was concerned. Now he wouldn't be saddled with guilt over walking away from a wasteland of a woman because he wouldn't have to know. Or saddled with staying for the same reason. "I didn't mean for it to end like this between us, Paul."

"Yes, you did. You've told me all along that I was only a

colleague to you, and that you only wanted my professional services. You have those now, Solange. And that's all there is."

"Paul, please—"

"I've got to go," he said, standing and heading to the door. "Bijou has the test results for you." Then he was gone, leaving Solange alone in his office, trying to hold back the tears until she could get back to the privacy of her truck.

She deserved this, and she wasn't angry with Paul for being so angry with her. But it did hurt much more than she could have possibly known it would.

"Get inside!" Solange yelled to Ayida. "And tell Frère Léon to see that the storm shutters are all in place. I'm going over to the infirmary to secure it, then I'm going to make sure the donkeys are safe in the shed. Don't worry if I don't make it back to the chapel until the worst of it is over. I'll ride it out in the infirmary. Just be sure the three of you stay safe." The wind was picking up fiercely now, and the rain was coming down, but not so hard it was a worry yet.

She'd made it back to The Mission just before nightfall and had spent most of the night fretting. Paul's anger, her father's interference... Nothing there had induced sleep. Then this morning, as she'd been about to drag herself out to her first stop, the storm had started rolling in. It was difficult to gauge these things. This one had been predicted to be a tropical depression at first, then a storm. Eventually there had been talk of a hurricane, but closer to Haiti. "I know I wanted something to take my mind off my personal problems," she grumbled, securing the doors to the medicine cabinet, "but not this."

Bolting down the storm shutters, essentially throwing everything in the small building into total darkness as the electricity had flickered out with the wind a while ago, Solange decided to go back to the chapel. Alone in the dark with her thoughts wasn't the way she cared to pass her time. There were too many thoughts of Paul rattling around in her head for the hours in the dark, humid solitude she was about to endure, so she ran to the door, threw it open and stepped outside.

The rain was coming down in torrential gusts and two steps out the door it pounded her backwards, into the front wall of the infirmary. She still wanted to fight her way across to the chapel, but good sense was taking hold. It was too far away, with so much open area between here and there. Too dangerous out in the open like that. "Guess it's the infirmary after all."

She was almost back inside when Gertie let out a bray that cut right through the wailing wind. The donkeys! They hadn't been secured in the shed as she'd thought. Right now they were standing in the middle of an open pasture, still grazing and oblivious to the weather. And much too vulnerable to survive the storm.

She had to bring them to safety, or they might die!

Bracing herself against the wind, Solange pulled herself along the front of the infirmary, clutching at the boards of the wall, then on around to the side, one agonizingly slow step followed by another. She paused briefly, pushing herself flat against the boards when a small uprooted tree went flying by as easily as flower petals drifting on a gentle summer breeze.

"You'll be fine," she said to herself. She'd been through these storms before. Just never outside. And this was beginning to make her nervous. "I don't know, *maman*," she cried, ducking her face from the wind to grab a breath. As she turned her head, Solange noticed that the donkeys were fast disappearing into the dense gray sheets of rain. This was getting to be a dire situation, because if the storm didn't kill them, they could die of fright for sure.

She was putting herself at risk, though. The same risk as the donkeys. And the chapel? It was a sound structure that had survived a century of this. At least her friends inside were safe. And smart, for not being out here in the gale.

"Just get Gertie," she said, trying to bolster her courage. "Get Gertie and the others will follow." Such a simple thing, really. Walk right out there, grab her and bring her back. Except that rain was stinging Solange's skin like shards of glass, and the intensity of the storm was increasing so quickly, and with so much fury, she could barely draw a breath. It was probably the same for the donkeys, she thought. Perhaps worse, since they weren't sheltered by the infirmary on one side.

"One try," she gasped. That's all she would have to get the donkeys. Only one try, and after that she had to think of her own life. "Gertie," she yelled, as she stepped away from the building, hoping that the donkey might come to her voice. "Come here, sweetie. Come on…" The wind slapped the rest of her words right back in her face, and she had to duck her head away from the force again to catch a breath.

Solange attempted her second steps out from the wall, but once again the wind caught her, knocking her right back into the wooden frame, so hard this time it punched the breath right out of her.

In the struggle to breathe again, her head started to go light, then she could feel a tingle spreading through her limbs as the result of lack of oxygen. At that moment, if she'd had enough breath to scream Paul's name, to beg him to come and help her, she would have. But he was long gone, and safe. Right now he was sitting in his office, looking out the window at the storm... In was a nice picture of him in her mind for that instant, and she closed her eyes to keep it from leaving her. "Paul...I do love you," she whispered, as the tears overtook her; tears of sadness more than fright.

Then suddenly, as if Paul had come to fight for her, she was able to take in a breath. Then another and another. Finally, when she was sufficiently sure she could breathe normally enough to have one more go at rescuing the donkeys, she turned to the pasture, only to find that they had wandered over to her and were waiting there, as if they were ready to be led away.

Minutes later, once Solange was safely inside the infirmary, along with the donkeys, she headed straight to one of the beds and cried herself to sleep.

"It's stopped," Solange commented to Gertie. She'd had a good long sleep through it all, which she'd so badly needed, and now it was time to go outside, see what kind of damage had been done, if any, and start the clean-up. That's the way it always worked after a storm. Get rid of what was destroyed, fix what could be fixed, and call Étoué and some of the others to come and help, if there was a need. Which there usually was. "Looks like you three are going back to the pasture, pronto." And none too soon, judging from the mess on the floor.

As she stepped outside, what struck her first was that it was so still. Nothing stirred. There were no sounds.

Immediately, Solange bolted to the side of the infirmary to assess the entire area and— "No!" she choked, frozen in a moment existing in that abyss somewhere between total reality and surreal terror. The chapel! It had collapsed in on itself. It was a pile of rubble, and her friends... *"Mon Dieu!"*

she screamed, breaking loose from the abyss and taking off at a dead run to the pile of debris.

Three of the exterior walls were still standing, but the roof had collapsed almost completely around them. "Ayida," she screamed. "Keskeya! Frère Léon?"

"Ayida and Keskeya are safe," Paul called, stepping out from behind a pile of rubble. "I haven't found Frère Léon yet."

"He's in the rubble?" Solange cried.

Paul nodded, then directed Étoué and several men from his village to begin carefully on a pile of rubble that would have been the kitchen. "I've had Ayida and Keskeya both taken back to the hospital only minutes ago. They were shaken up pretty badly, with some scrapes and bruises, but nothing serious."

She still didn't understand. "I don't…"

"I was on my way back here, Solange. Yesterday, after that whole nasty scene between us… I didn't want to leave it at that. I'd made it as far as Étoué's village when the storm hit, and he said it was worse farther up the mountain, that this kind of storm always was."

"And you didn't wake me up when you got here?"

"Wake you up? Hell, I thought you might be buried in all this mess with Frère Léon. Ayida and Keskeya were both hysterical, and I couldn't understand them…" He shrugged, then ran to her and pulled her into his arms. "Damn it, Solange. I was scared to death."

"We've got to find him, Paul," she choked. It was such a huge pile of debris, and Frère Léon could be anywhere. She only hoped that, wherever that was, he was still alive.

"I've only been here a few minutes, and we've barely begun looking. So let's start at the front. Étoué and his men are at the rear."

Solange nodded numbly. Without a word she grabbed up the first of hundreds of wooden shingles and tossed it aside. Then another and another, as Paul went to the side of the structure to do the same "Frère Léon," she called. "It's Solange. Hold on. Paul's here, and we'll get you out of there in just a minute. Can you hear me? We're going to get you out of there. Just listen to my voice…"

Her voice. Ten minutes later she was nearly hoarse from yelling. Through the entire ordeal, she talked to Frère Léon, reminding him of things they'd done together, teasing him about his love of good food, especially the sweets. As she ripped at the boards until her fingers were bleeding, pulling them away from the piles of debris and starting new piles with them, to listen to her would have given the impression that Frère Léon was right there at her side, participating in the conversation with her.

"And that day at the monastery when I made those horrible yeast rolls and all the brothers ate them simply to be polite. You were the only one who told me they weren't fit to throw to the chickens, and you were the only one who didn't make a pretense of even taking a second bite merely to spare my feelings. But I've been practicing when you go away. Did you know that? I can make a yeast roll now that doesn't taste like goat chow." She swiped at a tear, pulled up a large piece of wood and tossed it away. "And you're going to be the first one to try one, just as soon as we…" Solange's voice broke, and she shut her eyes, swallowed hard, and took in a deep breath. "Just as soon as we get you out of there."

Paul's heart ached for her. Trying to be so brave when she

was so scared. "I'm all the way down to the floor over here," he called, wishing desperately he could stop for a moment just to hold her. But he couldn't, of course. "I'm going to move a little further forward."

"No," Solange called. "That would be the women's showers, and he wouldn't have gone in there, no matter what."

They were a good fifteen minutes into the search now, and Paul was beginning to have grave doubts. If Frère Léon had been seriously injured, he could have bled to death by now. Or been smothered. There were too many scenarios he could think of that ended in tragedy. "Look, I'm going to the back for a minute to see how the others are coming. Will you be OK here alone?"

Instead of answering him, she nodded, then returned to plucking boards and shingles and pieces of broken furniture from the stacks of debris. "You saved my life," she whispered. "When I came to you, I really didn't care if I lived or died. It was all so bad for me then, Frère Léon, and I don't know what I would have done without you."

Paul hesitated at the side of the demolished structure as he heard her words. It was an intrusion, listening to something so private. But he couldn't pull himself away because there was so much about Solange he didn't know, so much that Frère Léon did.

"And after I was feeling better, and you began to tell me about the needs of these wonderful people living here on the mountain... I'd been here to the mountain so often with my mother, and I didn't know, yet you knew that's what I needed, didn't you? You knew that's what I needed to make me whole again. I'm not there yet, and I'm trying very hard. You've got to be there when I come through this. And I will. I promise, I will. And you'll be there with me."

Paul stepped away, cursing himself for listening. As much as he wanted to know everything, it couldn't be this way.

Even though it felt like an eternity, by the time Paul had returned to the front of the structure, they'd been at the search seventeen minutes. Seventeen futile minutes, and Solange was now at the end of her first pile, looking at the bare wooden floor of what had once been the vestibule. Solange stood up straight for a moment, stretched, and looked around, then stepped across to another pile of debris and started all over again. Fighting with every ounce of strength in her, she ripped at the boards, talking non-stop to Frère Léon until—"*Mon Dieu!*" she gasped. "Paul! Over here. I need help!"

Solange threw herself to her knees and started pulling frantically at the pieces of wood, one by one, afraid that if she moved too quickly it could cause an avalanche of debris to come crushing down on the monk. So she went cautiously, praying to herself and talking out loud to Frère Léon. "Wiggle your fingers," she said, to which there was no response. "Just one little wiggle. That's all I want."

Paul ran to her side, dropped to his knees and started the same arduous task. Within seconds an arm was revealed. Pasty skin, unmoving. Limp. Instinctively, Solange reached to feel for the pulse in his wrist... It was there, but very faint.

In mere seconds the other men had converged on the spot in which Frère Léon was trapped, and it took only a few seconds more before the debris was totally off him.

Immediately Solange assessed his pupillary reaction to ascertain brain damage, and thankfully it was normal. Paul was busy looking for obvious broken bones and other injuries. "His belly is fine," he said. "I don't think there's an internal bleed because his abdomen isn't rigid. But his left ankle is shattered. I think he's going to need surgery to fix it up, but other than the conk on his head and the ankle, I think our friend here is in decent shape, considering that the entire building collapsed on him."

"You're going to be fine," Solange finally whispered, her fingers entwined in Frère Léon's. She reached up to swipe at her tears, then smiled over at Paul. "Did you hear me, Frère Léon? You're going to be just fine."

CHAPTER ELEVEN

"HE'S holding on pretty well, all things considered, and not too grumpy because I won't give him anything stronger than an aspirin."

"You explained that his bump on the head..."

Paul nodded. "Bump on the head and going in and out of consciousness like he's still doing, I told him that refusing him pain pills is standard medical protocol, and I really hate to do that because I know his ankle is killing him." Paul dropped down onto one of the two straight-backed metal chairs against the wall, leaned his head back, and shut his eyes. Then he let out a deep, weary breath. "And he said to tell you the yeast rolls didn't taste like goat chow."

"He said that?"

Paul nodded. "Cardboard. I think his exact words were 'burnt cardboard soaked in tar drippings'."

"And here I offered to bake him more. See what kind of gratitude I get for that." Solange laughed as she strolled over to the door separating the two rooms and looked in at Frère Léon. He was sleeping again, as he had been off and on for the past hour. "We need to get him out of here," she said. "Normally, he'd be the one I'd rely on to find a way."

"You need to come here, sit down, and leave that to Étoué. He'll find a way to get help up here." He patted the chair next to him.

Under different circumstances she might have moved her chair to the other side of the room, but that seemed silly now. Everything seemed silly, considering what they'd just gone through.

"I heard some of what you were saying to him," Paul confessed. "And I'm sorry for listening, but..." He shrugged. "I did."

"Which part?" She'd said so many things in those interminable minutes she wasn't sure she remembered all she'd told Frère Léon.

"About how he saved your life during a bad time, and that you're not over it yet. Was it about Mauricio?"

"Not really. He was simply the catalyst, I think. I had other issues—family, career, personal, and Mauricio simply exacerbated the situation."

"And sent you off to have a breakdown?"

"Sounds so bad, doesn't it? A breakdown... Solange Léandre had a breakdown. It was more of an emotional retreat, I think, and Mauricio didn't send me off to have it. I did. I needed space, and Frère Léon had it to offer me. And it was nice to have support at a very difficult time in my life."

"Your father didn't support you?"

"My father's support consisted of telling me Mauricio wasn't the man he would have chosen for me and I was better off without him. Which I was, although I certainly wasn't in an emotional place to tell him he'd been correct." She shook her head. "He has an impossible standard for the men in my life...and my sister's."

"Because when he sees the men in your life, or your sister's, he's thinking in terms of a grandson."

"I know that!" she snapped. "That's all I've heard since I was old enough to..." To what? Have children? That window of opportunity had opened when she'd been twelve and had stopped when she'd been thirty-one. Nineteen years seemed like an eternity in so many ways, yet like such a short time in so many others. "Something my mother did not give him. A male heir. My duty to uphold the family name. That's not where I want to be but, of course, that's exactly what he wants from me. Maybe the only thing he wants."

"Where *do* you want to be, and don't tell me right here because this is only a place. Where do you want to be in your life? I've been trying to figure that out all this time, and every time I get near, you seem to skirt around it. We were friends. We were more than friends. Then we were nothing. And I have to know why. It's driving me crazy because I don't believe you're the kind of woman who would be so cavalier about a relationship. Which is what you were with us. You wanted what we had, then you walked away from it when you realized that I wanted it, too. And I really had to do some soul-searching to get to that point."

"And you think I didn't?" she snapped, springing up from her chair.

He caught her by the arm, then stood up. "I have a right to know."

"No, you don't. In my life, you have *no* rights. And don't think that because you came up here to make up, that's going to change things between us. You want from me what my father expects from me. He rejected you when he thought there was something between us because you weren't settled enough, but that's what you would do to me, Paul. *Settle me.* You said it in so many words, and I don't want to be settled."

"I never said *anything* about trying to settle you, Solange. I would never ask you to give up doing what you want to do."

"No, you wouldn't. But you talked about changing your lifestyle in a couple of years when the hospital is better funded, and in that scenario you had me having babies..." She yanked her arm free of him. "So how can you tell me that you don't want to settle me, Paul? Babies do that. Husbands do that! And I can't," she cried. "I just can't!"

"But you were willing to do that with Mauricio?"

"I was younger then. My life was completely different. *I was completely different!*" She fled to the infirmary door, opened it and ran outside, only to be slammed by the ruins yet again. Ruins. The symbol of her life. "I should have never let us get to the point we did, Paul," she said, as he followed her out. "You and me—we both knew there couldn't be any more than a casual acquaintance, and I'm so sorry it went past that for you. I never meant for it to happen that way. I never meant to hurt you."

"Do you still love him, Solange?" Paul asked. "Is that what this is about? Do you still love Mauricio?"

She laughed sadly. "The truth is, I never loved him. Never even came close." Loving Paul had taught her that.

Solange drew in a breath of pure Kijé air. Funny, how something as destructive as the storm had a healing power to it. The chapel was gone, but the dead wood had been blown from the trees, making way for new growth, and the impurities blown from the air had made way for a renewal of purity. This was nature renewing itself to start afresh.

If only it was that easy.

* * *

"You should be going after her now," Frère Léon said, as Paul stepped into the tiny infirmary.

Paul dropped down onto the bed across from the monk, and lay flat on his back to look up at the rough-hewn boards of the ceiling. "Right now, I think that's the last thing she wants," he said.

"Or the only thing she wants." Frère Léon rubbed his hand over the bandage under which the IV line was anchored. "Did I thank you for saving my life, Paul?"

"I heard Solange thank you for saving hers."

"And she'll tell you about it when she's able."

"Or not." He huffed out an exasperated breath. "Her father doesn't want me with her because I'm not settled enough to settle her, and he thinks I'll..." Paul raised his head and glanced over at the monk. "If I confess something to you, you can't tell anyone, can you? I'm not sure how that works with a monk."

Frère Léon chuckled. "I would never violate a sacred trust. But I think I already know what you were going to tell me. Monsieur Léandre is afraid that you will cheat on his daughter, the way he cheated on his wife."

"Did he confess that to you?" Paul asked incredulously.

"Just an educated guess. He is a man who has endured a heavy heart for as many years as I've known him, and I have seen that in him constantly. Because he has a successful life, successful businesses, successful daughters, the only reason for that heavy heart could be something where he was not a success, and since his wife was truly all that really mattered to him, my guess is that he failed her."

"As he thinks I will fail Solange because my lifestyle would not be so dissimilar from his, always separated, if Solange and

I were ever to... And he threatened to pull out the funding for the hospital if anything happens between us."

"And you expected that he wouldn't threaten you? He's a man who's used to getting his own way, and the only thing he knows to do is use his power. But he has a sensible head. He won't hurt the hospital, especially if you re-name it after his beloved Gabriella. And since you have no ego in this matter..."

Paul grinned. "You *are* a tricky devil, aren't you?"

"Experienced. There's more of me than meets the eye than my brown robes." He smiled. "Whatever Monsieur Léandre has done is his grief to bear, Paul. You, however, are not Monsieur Léandre, and you have no leanings in that direction."

"Well, it doesn't matter to Solange what kind of leanings I have, because she doesn't want me, and she couldn't be any clearer about that. So maybe I should just take the rather obvious hint and move on, because this is just becoming so damned frustrating. I fell in love with her the first time I laid eyes on her. Did you know that?"

"I knew that you would. How could you not?"

"How could I not, indeed! And I've told her that I wouldn't expect her to change her life, to settle down the way Bertrand expects her to. Settle down, have a grandson for him. I even said that if we ever were to have children, I'd be glad to stay home while she goes off to the mountain..."

"Children?" Frère Lèon choked, and immediately Paul was at his bedside, listening first to Frère Léon's heart then to his lungs. "You need to rest," he said, pulling the stethoscope out of his ears and setting it on top of the bedside stand. "No more matchmaking for you for some time to come, and that's an order." He took a deep breath to steady himself.

"Dammit, Léon, you scared the hell out of me out there in the chapel when Solange and I thought you were—"

"Will I be able to get back out there to the mountain?" he asked, his voice noticeably weaker.

Paul sat down on the side of the bed and took hold of Frère Léon's hand. "Maybe not in the way you did before. But you'll make it, and I want you to trust me on this. You're going to be fine."

"Then you have to trust me on this, Paul. Solange is worth the effort." He gave Paul a faint smile and a wink, then shut his eyes to nap.

"A helicopter?" Paul asked, standing on the porch.

Solange looked up at it, as shocked as Paul was. Sure enough, there was a helicopter, getting ready to set down on the grass, its blades blowing up dust, the roar of its rotors nearly deafening.

"It looks to me like there are still miracles," she replied, watching the pilot maneuver the mechanical bird to the ground. "So, now that we have a ride out of here, where do we take Frère Léon?" she asked. "Back to your hospital?"

Paul shook his head. "To the orthopaedic care center in Port Georges. He needs the best, and I don't have the proper facilities for long-term rehabilitation, which is what he's going to need."

She laughed. "Isn't that how all this started? I came to you because I didn't have the facilities?" She waved at her father as he stepped out of the helicopter and crossed the compound. She wasn't surprised it was him. If there ever was anybody who could conjure up a miracle like this, it was Bertrand Léandre.

"I got here as quickly as I could," Bertrand yelled over the noise of the helicopter. "One of the villagers went to Dr Sebastian who, in turn, called me for help to evacuate Frère Léon. How is he, by the way?"

"Holding his own, Papa," Solange said, stepping into her father's embrace. "It's a serious injury, but not grave."

"And you were not injured?"

"No, Papa. I was in the infirmary when the storm hit, and it's a much newer, much stronger structure than the old chapel was." She waited until he had kissed her on top of her head before she stepped away. "All things considered, we were very lucky that no one was killed."

"He's ready to go," Paul shouted to Bertrand. "And I'd like to get him to Port Georges right away, so he can still have surgery today. Can you radio ahead to the hospital once we're *en route*?"

"Of course," Bertrand said, stepping past Solange. "Do you have a stretcher, *mon ami*?"

Five minutes later, Solange stood back as her father and Paul lifted Frère Léon into the helicopter. Paul righted the IV set-up, made sure the oxygen cylinder was full enough to last the trip, then ran back over to Solange. "There's only room for one of us, so you go to Port Georges with him," he said. "I'll hike down and catch up with you there, probably some time tomorrow."

"Tell my father I said thank you for doing this," Solange said. Then she turned around and went into the infirmary, shut the door, and locked it.

"Solange!" Paul shouted. "This is crazy. You can't stay here alone."

Her back to the door, she shut her eyes, trying to pretend that if she couldn't see it, it did not exist. But it did. She saw it, she felt it, she heard it. This was where she would walk away from Paul. He would go to Port Georges in a few minutes. And they would resume the lives they'd had before they'd met. "Go away," she whispered, brushing back the tears beginning to slide down her cheeks.

"Come on, Solange. You go with your father and Frère Léon."

"Go away," she whispered again.

"Solange…"

Solange didn't open the door until the helicopter had lifted off. She watched it from the infirmary window until it was a but a tiny speck in the sky. Then she grabbed up her backpack and began to fill it with her traveling necessities. "So this where I start over again, *maman*." Once the pack was full, she locked the door behind her and headed up the path to the first village on her rounds.

"I don't know about resting for another three months," Frère Léon said, gingerly swinging his legs over the side of the bed. "That's all I've been doing these past three weeks, and frankly I'm tired of it. Although the nurses are pretty, I will say."

"Are you supposed to be looking at the nurses like that?" Paul asked, helping Frère Léon adjust his feet to the floor. The monk was in a flimsy hospital gown, one white support stocking and a single blue scuffy for his right foot as his left was in a cast up to the knee. The surgery had turned out to be far less invasive than it could have been: a few pins in his ankle for support, and he had been practically good to go—at least for several trips up and down the corridor daily.

"I'm celibate, not dead." He laughed. "Speaking of which…"

Paul shook his head. "Not a word. I know she's out there,

but I haven't been able to catch up with her. With my schedule I don't have much time to go out and look for her, and when I do manage a few hours, she's either just been through the village or they have no idea when she'll come around."

"She's lost a lot in her life," Frère Léon said, pulling on a hospital robe to cover the gaping back of his gown, then grabbing up his metal walker. "She needs time, and Solange has an odd way of working these things out."

"These things." Paul snorted. "I have no idea what *these things* are."

"I expect that being in love with you is one of them." Frère Léon winked at one of the nurses lumbering sluggishly through the hall pushing a medicine cart ahead of her. She was an older woman with an unfriendly scowl on her face and obviously at odds with her life. She lit up at Frère Léon's approach then walked away, smiling. "Wilhelmina there is a lovely woman, really. She just needs someone to coax it out of her."

"But sometimes it's just too risky. I've tried to coax it out of Solange but she's scared to death of the risk."

Frère Léon stopped and spun cautiously to face Paul, taking care not to bear down too much on his bad ankle. "Life is about risk. Every step you take is a risk, and every step you don't take an even bigger risk. I don't know where my steps will take me just yet, but at least I'm willing to take them. And right now, as you can see, I need help in doing that, just as you do."

"It always gets back to Solange, doesn't it?" Paul said, his voice full of sadness.

"Does an hour ever go by that you don't squeeze in a thought or two of her?"

Paul shook his head. "I admitted that I love her, so thinking about her is natural."

"You love her, and here you are, wandering up and down the hall with me." Frère Léon shook his head. "I'd suggest you go take a little risk yourself. The sooner the better, since it's time for me to wander over to the vending machine and see what candy bar I'll be risking today."

Paul gave him a hug. "If it's appropriate for one man to hug another and tell him that he loves him, that's what I'm doing here. Because I do love you, and I want you to come stay with me in Abbeville once they let you out of here. It's not the hike in the mountains you want, but I do promise you something close to it."

Wilhelmina scooted by the two men, casting them a dubious glance.

"I might just do that, Paul," Frère Lèon said. "I might just do that."

It didn't look much different than it had every time Paul had come through the past several weeks. Empty. No life whatsoever. He knew Solange came back here for supplies, and that her father did continue to send fresh medical supplies up. But she was never here when Paul arrived, and perhaps he hadn't stayed to wait for her because he was afraid of what might happen when they did finally meet again.

"It *is* time," he said aloud, as he sat down on the floor of the infirmary porch. "One way or another, it is time." He certainly could not go on like this, loving Solange the way he did and not knowing why she kept running from him. Actually, running from everything. He'd been patient. No questions asked about the time she'd stayed at the monastery with the brothers, no questions asked about her special relationship with Frère Léon. Pretty much no questions asked at all, because he respected her privacy, and he truly believed that in time she would be forthright with him. Or he'd hoped so, anyway.

So now he was going to wait it out. No turning back because she wasn't there. It was time.

Almost home. Solange couldn't wait to sleep in her own bed that night. Maybe two nights. She was tired now. Constantly on the move for over three weeks tended to do that. But the good thing was, she didn't have much time to think in between her stops. And the villagers were genuinely pleased to see her when she arrived. Several had volunteered to build another structure here—a place to live. Some had offered timber and other goods. "It's going to work, *maman*," she said. "So many people want to help." And as soon as she had shelter, Ayida and Keskeya would come back to her. She'd run into them in one of the villages and they were eager.

She wasn't sure about Frère Léon, however. She hadn't gone to see him. Actually, she hadn't gone off the mountain at all. But word spread quickly, and where Frère Léon was concerned, word about him was good. He was making a good recovery, and she would definitely go to see him once he returned to the monastery to recuperate. At least, she assumed he would return to the monastery.

Of course, he could come back here, too. Perhaps when things were built back up, he would and she could help him find his way back, as he had done for her.

At the edge of the compound, Solange stopped to look at the rubble. It was still there, the way it had been the day the chapel had collapsed. It always made her catch her breath, seeing it like that. Of course, she knew it was there, yet it never failed to give her a shock. Then, as always, after the reminder of what had happened to the chapel, her next thought was of Paul. She missed him so badly, and she had actually headed toward Abbeville more times than she could count over the weeks, only to turn around when good sense had prevailed. Absence might make the heart grow fonder for a while, but in time he would get over his feelings for her. Maybe he was now. Maybe he was so angry with her that everything else was gone from him.

She didn't see him on the porch until she was almost there. He was sitting in the shadows, sleeping, looking scruffy, like he hadn't shaved in days. Her first thought was to tiptoe away before he woke up. If he'd been staying there, waiting for her, his schedule would eventually pull him back to Abbeville, then on to destinations unknown.

That would have been the smart thing to do, but just watching the rise and fall of his chest and listening to the gentle little snore… She ached so badly from missing him that pain of it paralyzed her. She couldn't move, couldn't run away. And maybe she didn't want to.

"Paul," she whispered, setting down her pack and stepping up onto the porch. "How long have you been waiting here?"

"Three days," he said, without opening his eyes.

Three days. He'd been waiting here on the porch for three days. The thought of it made her want to cry, but she had to find that hard exterior and get herself into it immediately, before what she truly wanted slipped right out. *For Paul*, she told herself. "I'd think you'd have better things to do with your time," she replied, hoping it sounded appropriately stiff.

Solange stepped past him, unlocked the infirmary door, went inside, and closed the door behind her. Then she almost melted into the floor. This was so difficult. But she had to end it here. Once, and for always.

CHAPTER TWELVE

"Do you really think shutting the door is going to keep me out?" Paul shouted.

Solange ran into the other room, shut that door, then stood with her back to it. Her breaths were coming in bursts now, and her hands were trembling. The frightened rabbit running away from the wildcat. If the rabbit was quick enough, or found a sufficiently deep burrow, it would live to run another day. If not, the wildcat had its meal.

So why did she feel like she was standing in the middle of a big pot of rabbit stew?

"Come on, Solange," he yelled, this time from the next room. "I'm sure you want to hear all about Frère Léon."

"He's fine," she replied. "I've had word."

"He's worried about you."

"He knows I'm capable of taking care of myself." Her knees were shaking now. The heat was turning up on that stew pot, and she wished to heaven she'd had a back door built in this infirmary. "Paul, go away. Whatever you think it was we had between us, it wasn't."

"Are you sure?" He was just on the other side of the door now.

"It was sex, Paul. That's all. Just sex. One night. One-night stand."

"Are you sure?" he asked again.

"I told you the first night we met that—"

He pulled the door open and she practically fell into his arms. Once she'd recovered, she scrambled away from him to the opposite side of the room. "I told you the first night we met that I liked my life the way it is. And the way it is, Paul, is without you in it. You were a nice diversion, and I'd hoped that we might be friends, but you took it too far. You're taking it too far right now, coming here like this, waiting for me to return. That's crazy!"

He nodded. "I agree. It's quite crazy, considering how the woman I love resists me at every turn."

"So why do you keep coming back when you know what I'll do?"

"Actually, I've been asking myself the same question for the past three days. And I've got to tell you it's bloody boring up here all alone. But I knew you'd return eventually so I waited until you did. Which gave me lots of time to think." He took two steps toward her and she took two steps backwards. "And it wasn't sex, Solange." He chuckled. "Well, maybe in the technical sense, that's what you could call it. But on my part, it was making love to the woman I love. Does that make you uncomfortable, hearing it put like that? That you're the woman I love? That's what I've been telling myself, over and over these past three days while I was waiting. That I love you and you're worth fighting my way through this hell you're putting me through."

She took another step backwards. "You can call it what you like, but that doesn't change the facts between us."

"What facts, Solange? That you don't love me?" He took a step forward.

"That this will not work between us. You want one thing, I want another." She sidestepped over to the medicine cabinet, then slipped to the side of it, pressing her back to the wall.

"If you're talking professionally, I believe we want the same things. We just go about accomplishing them differently, which isn't a problem. I'll have my schedule, you'll have yours, and we'll have ours. And we can do that, Solange. We're both strong enough to know that we don't have to fit into the typical mold. And who knows? Situations change. We may want to make a new mold together in a year or two. Something where we are together more often."

"Doing what, Paul? We're together more often, doing what?"

"Doing whatever it is that married couples do, I suppose. Married couples in our situation, anyway."

"Like starting a family, putting baby photos in the picture album, taking Paul Junior to play baseball in the Little League?"

He walked over to her corner and stopped short of it by only two feet, then reached out to brush a tear off her cheek. "Tell me, Solange. I have to know."

"There's nothing to know," she said, slapping his hand away. The defiance in her was dying, the hard exterior slipping away.

"Are you afraid of a relationship like your parents had? Is that what it is?"

"My parents dealt with their situation, and what they had worked for them," she said, casting her eyes to the floor.

Paul drew in a ragged breath, then reached out to brush another tear from her cheek. "So tell me," he said, his voice so tender it broke her heart.

"Tell you what, Paul? That I don't want a relationship with you? I thought I'd already said that."

"Tell me that you don't love me." He titled her head up with his fingertips. "Look into my eyes and tell me that you don't love me. If you're telling the truth, I'll leave, and I won't bother you again."

She looked up into those eyes, those beautiful blue eyes, and prayed she could lie convincingly. "I don't…" She swallowed hard. "I can't…" Then she shut her eyes, drew in a steadying breath, and opened them again. "Paul, I don't…"

"Yes," he whispered. "You do. So tell me, Solange."

She swiped back a tear and nodded. There was no other way. Paul would not leave her until he knew. So she would tell him her story and pray that pity, or honor, or sense of duty didn't stop him from leaving.

Solange took in a calming breath, then began. "I'd been with Mauricio a year when I started feeling bad. Nothing serious, mostly tired. But with my work schedule I didn't think much about it. Then my periods got heavy and irregular, and I'd have cramps that would double me over." She stepped away from the wall, going over to the window. Turning her back to Paul, she looked out over the compound to the ruins of the chapel. "It was endometriosis, which didn't surprise me because the symptoms were classic. When I told Mauricio what it was, he looked at me with revulsion."

"Because he was a fool." Paul stepped up and wrapped his arms around her. "A damn fool."

"I struggled for nearly two years with it, until I couldn't bear it any more and I had a hysterectomy. I was thirty-one, Paul. No babies for Solange. Not ever."

"And the jerk left you because of that?"

"I left him. He wanted children that I couldn't have, and suddenly the whole life we were building wasn't good enough for him. It took me a while to realize that it wasn't the life that was not good enough. It was me. I ceased to be good enough when my ovaries were removed."

"He wasn't good enough for you, using something like that as an excuse to push you away."

"It wasn't an excuse, Paul. He wanted children. You want children, too. You've said that over and over, in many ways."

"No wonder you wouldn't let me kiss your belly that night."

"My scar...always the reminder," she said sadly.

"So let me get this straight. You can't have kids and you knew that I wanted them so you decided to make a grand sacrifice by turning me away for my own good. Admit it, Solange. Isn't that what you were doing?"

Solange spun around to face him. "Yes, that's exactly what I was doing. And nothing has changed. Right now, you're thinking that my *condition* doesn't matter, that you love me no matter what. Which turns you into the one making a grand sacrifice since I know what you want, Paul."

"That is a pretty grand sacrifice, isn't it," he snapped, running his hand angrily through his hair, "for a man who wants a breeding machine, as you think that I do?"

"Stop it, Paul. Don't make light of this."

"But that's what you're doing, Solange. Making light of it. *Making light of me.* Isn't it? By not allowing me into the decision, by not telling me what's motivating your decision...your decision *for me*, that is making light of everything." He thundered across the wooden boards of the floor to the two metal chairs lined up against the wall, and kicked the first one he came to. "That's your father, Solange. Don't you see that? You're trying to control the situation to the outcome you want, just the way he does. Always trying to manipulate the situation in the way he...or in this case *you*...think is best for the other person."

"It *is* best for you, and someday you'll see that."

"Says you!" he shouted.

"Yes, says me." She swallowed hard, fighting to stay calm, fighting not to cry. This was harder than she'd thought it would be. He should have heard the pronouncement and walked away. But to fight her?

That's why she loved him. He was passionate about his desires. And they weren't selfish, like the desires of every other man she'd ever had in her life. Her father, Mauricio, even her one-time date with the chocolates and champagne. There was nothing in Paul that could be selfish. "You're an honorable man, Paul, and an honorable man would do the honorable thing. But given the proximity of what our relationship would be if we..."

She paused, shoved her hair away from her face, and squeezed shut her eyes for a second, trying to get hold of her nerves. "Our relationship, you traveling in one direction and me in another, and with all your hopes and dreams pinned to settling down with a wife and children someday..." Solange opened her eyes and turned to face Paul. "Don't you see? You even said you'd raise those children so I could keep doing the kind of doctoring up in the mountains I want to do. You might delude yourself at first that this could work, that we could live happily ever after in our own strange way, but eventually you would come to resent me, maybe even hate me."

"Because you can't have children?" His voice softened. "Do you really believe I'm that shallow, Solange?"

"Not shallow, Paul. Realistic. You said you and Joanna

might have had a stronger bond if you'd had children, that the outcome of your marriage might have been different."

"Of course it would have been different and, yes, there would have been a stronger bond. Would our marriage have survived, though?" He shrugged. "I don't know. It might have gone on a while longer. But it might have ended as it did. There's no use speculating on what might have been because all that's in the past."

"Like my ability to bear children."

"Dammit, Solange. I don't care about that." He stepped forward to pull her into his arms, but she placed the palms of her hands on his chest and shoved him away.

"My father wanted his legacy, Paul. He never had a son, and he still wants one, or at least a grandson. He's passionate to continue the Léandre line with the male heir that my mother didn't give him. Even Mauricio, as shallow as he was, wanted the same thing. And so do you…a dozen of them, in your own words."

"Dumb words," Paul said. "And I'm so sorry."

"Not dumb. Honest." Solange opened the door and stepped outside. The small infirmary was becoming too confining. "I had a breakdown, Paul. You know that already. That's when I went to stay with Frère Léon. After the hysterectomy I couldn't cope with all the changes, so I went away for a while."

"Hormones?"

She nodded. "Hormone surges and finality. A punch for which no one is ever prepared."

Paul stepped up behind Solange and wrapped his arms around her. "I wish I'd been there to help you through it."

The feel of his arms around her was so good, and she ached

to deceive herself that she could stay there, just like they were in that moment. But that was merely a delusion. He would fight passionately for her now, but in the end, after a year, after five years... "There are so many things that can pull even the strongest bond apart. My parents had a strong bond, yet my father cheated on my mother. And he did love her, I've never doubted that. But the life they lived took a horrible toll, and I can still remember all the lady visitors to our guest house when Papa was alone and Maman was in Paris. That was a *strong* marriage he was cheating on, Paul. One he truly wanted and believed in."

"Because he was a weak man," Paul said. "In the end, for all your father's outward strength, he's a weak and very sad man over it. I think it will haunt him the rest of his life."

She pushed out of his arms and spun to face him. "You knew?"

"He told me weeks ago when he warned me away from you. He believes I would do the same to you, given the way we would lead our lives. And, yes, he does want to see you settled and having babies, and he says I'm not settled enough to settle you." He pulled her back into his arms. "But I wouldn't cheat on you, Solange! If that's what you're afraid of, I would never cheat."

"I know you wouldn't," she whispered. "But I'm so frightened of that look on your face when you realize, one day, that you need more than I am. Paul, I couldn't bear that."

Two children wandered through the door, waving at Paul. "Hacky sack," one of them called, holding up one of the bean bags Paul had brought weeks earlier. "Hacky sack, please, *Doktè!*"

"Go play hacky sack," Solange said.

"I don't want to leave you."

"I'm not going anywhere, Paul. This is where I belong." She stepped off the porch and headed to the donkey shed. Gertie and Pete and Lulu were down with Ràfer Babin right now. But she needed to get away from Paul, and going anywhere was better than staying.

What have I done? Paul asked himself as he kicked the hacky sack to the smaller of the two boys. Solange loved him. He knew that with all his heart. But she was so frightened...frightened by the things her father had done, by the way Mauricio had treated her and, yes, even by him, by the things he'd said.

"She should have told me," he said to the boys, who clearly did not understand him. "Instead of hiding it from me like it was an embarrassment, she should have told me. Of course, I didn't exactly make that easy for her, did I, with all that talk of wanting children?"

The older of the two boys tossed the hacky sack straight up in the air and Paul snatched it with his hand, then tossed it over to the younger of the boys to start the next round of play. Squealing with delight, the child lifted his knee and totally missed the bean bag, then dove to the ground to get it before his playmate could. The older boy dove at the same time, and the two of them tussled about in the grass for a few moments, before Paul swooped in, grabbed the hacky sack then held it high for the boys to jump at and try to grab from his hand.

Yes, he did love children. And the older he got, the more he realized that once he'd finished this part of his life—the part where he was a road warrior, always going out to look for funds—he wanted to settle back into being a doctor again, but a doctor for children with infectious diseases. A small specialty that he'd been thinking about since he'd met Tsombé. That was still quite a while into the future, but something he wanted, almost as much as he wanted Solange.

"I love you," he shouted at the donkey shed, as he lowered the hacky sack enough to let the younger of the boys grab it. "And nothing has changed. I want to marry you, Solange."

Of course she didn't answer. It would have been nice if she'd heard his words and come running straight into his arms. But that wasn't Solange. Not at all. And all he got for his effort was a hacky sack kicked straight into his gut.

The boys, seeing what had just happened, backed away, wide-eyed and ready to run, but Paul held out the toy with one hand and invited them closer with the other. "Don't ever run away from challenges," he told them. "Especially not if something you want very badly is at the other end of the challenge."

Something you want very badly…

Solange!

"Look, boys, I've got to go take some of my advice. And it may take a while." He waved goodbye as he headed for the shed. It might take a while? Hell, it might take for ever. But this was what he wanted very badly, and Solange was at the other end of the challenge.

Solange ducked away from the shed window when she saw him coming straight there, and grabbed a pitchfork to shuffle up the straw. "I don't know what to do, *maman*," she whispered. "He says it doesn't matter that I cannot give him children, and maybe right now it doesn't, but…I just don't know."

She tossed the straw angrily into a pile in the corner, her back to the door when Paul stepped inside.

"Will you marry me?" he asked.

She didn't turn around to face him. Couldn't.

"Solange, I love you, and you love me. At least be decent enough to admit that much—that you love me. Because you do, and you cannot lie about it. Not to me, and not to yourself."

Please, maman! she begged.

"We might not always be together, but we would always be on the same mission, with the same goal, and that does make us close, Solange. Closer than most couples who live together every day, every night."

Maman!

"Will you at least answer a question for me?" Paul asked, stepping up behind her, his voice so quiet she could barely hear him.

She could feel his presence. Even if she hadn't known he'd been there, she would have felt him there—that little tingle that always shot up and down her arms, the quickening of her heartbeat, that slight catch in her breath. It's what she'd felt the first time she'd ever seen him and it's what she'd felt every time thereafter. "Yes," she choked, stabbing the pitchfork down into the straw.

"Do *you* want children, Solange? With all the argument and all the emotion over this whole mess, that's something I don't know about you. And it's something I have to know. So, please, don't tell me that you can't. Put everything aside for a moment and just tell me if you *want* children."

She steadied herself with a deep breath, flung another clump of straw into the corner, and nodded. "Yes," she whispered. "Very much." More now than she ever had before.

"With me?"

She nodded. "Only with you."

Paul shut his eyes and smiled. "There are many children to adopt, Solange."

"Not of your blood."

He chuckled. "You're not of my blood, but I love you more than my own life. Love isn't always about a blood connection. It's about heart. That's all." He reached around, took the pitchfork from her hands and tossed it onto the pile of straw, then wrapped his arms around her. "And you've got so much heart for everything and everyone. I know that if you want children it won't matter to you that they're not of your blood. That's not the kind of person you are. Any child who needs us will be ours Solange."

She leaned her head back to his shoulder. "I'm so scared," she said. "I do trust you and believe what you say, but—"

"Shh. That's all we need. For now. And I'm not going to rush you through this, Solange. I know you're dealing with many conflicts and, I promise, I'm not going to rush you into anything. But you've got to know, I love you, and I do want to marry you. That's not going to change, no matter if you're up on your mountain somewhere or I'm in Boston. *I love you.* And you can count on that."

Solange blinked back the tears. "I am being a bit like my father," she admitted.

"A bit? From where I'm watching this, you're behaving *awfully* like your father. But you're much cuter." He pulled her hair up and kissed her lightly on the neck.

"I want to rebuild here, Paul. A bigger and better infirmary. And maybe someday a cottage by the waterfall."

"Is there room for me in that cottage?"

"Yes, there is. But what about your hospital, Paul? You can't walk away from it."

"I don't intend to, like you don't intend to walk away from your mountain. That's who we are, Solange."

She turned to face him. "So is this where we start to live by the calendar, marking off the days when we're apart and marking in the days when we can be together?"

"If you'll have me, Solange, that's exactly how our life will be for now. And the rest of it doesn't matter. We'll figure it out as we go."

"I do trust you," she whispered. "More than that, I love you. And for now it sounds like a beautiful life, if you'll have me with all my ups and downs and hormonal fits."

"On one condition," he said.

"Which is?"

"Could I go have a closer look at that scar right now?"

Solange entwined her hands around Paul's neck and pulled his face down to hers. "Only if you'll let me examine you for scars, too," she whispered.

Paul sighed before he kissed her. "Examine away, Doctor."

"My pleasure, Doctor."

"It's for you. I couldn't afford it when we got married but I came across a great deal on the Internet."

The gift wasn't concealed well. Wrapped meticulously from the handle grip to the club, the paper molded right to it, and Solange beamed as Paul peeled the paper away, one strip at a time.

"A Ping Anser 2!" Paul exclaimed. "You remembered that?"

Solange laughed. "Actually, you told me several names that day and that was the only one I remembered. I hope it's right."

She grinned wickedly. "It was easier to buy once I knew the particulars of your measurements. That's very important in buying the perfect putter, you know."

Paul gripped the club and went through the motions of a putt. "Any time you want a measurement, just let me know. I'm more than happy to oblige."

"You didn't even know you were being measured, Doctor." Solange fished a golf ball from her pocket and handed it to him. "Care to putt for real?"

"You don't know how bad," he said, setting the putter aside and pulling her into his arms.

"Excuse me. Hate to interrupt here, but it's simply too small," Frère Léon said, whooshing into the room, cane in one hand, blueprints in the other. "Much too small, and I'm not going to approve it."

"And you're referring to what?" Paul chuckled.

"The children's ward of the Gabriella Bontecou Léandre Hospital, of course."

"That's such a nice name," Solange said, smiling. "Thank you, Paul. She would have loved the tribute."

"She would have loved the tribute, but not the small play area for the children," Frère Léon persisted. He slapped the plans down on Paul's desk. "I've reassigned the architect who designed this cubbyhole to designing a shed for Solange's kiln, since he seems to thrive in creating small spaces."

"You're doing that for me?" Solange choked, throwing her arms around Paul's neck and kissing him. "First the hospital name, then a pottery shed?"

Frère Léon glanced quickly at Solange, then at Paul, then slapped his forehead. "Did I spoil that surprise?" he asked.

Paul tossed him a fake frown over Solange's shoulder. "It's

tiny, Solange. We're going to build it with the leftovers from the building materials for the children's ward. And it won't be built until we see what's left."

"And I only bought you a putter."

"Not just any putter. You bought me a Ping Anser 2!"

"Ping Ansers and pottery kilns!" Frère Léon exclaimed. "I've got a ward to build, and an old friend on his way from Jamaica who insists on doing the design of this thing—and doing it the correct way. He'll be here in a day or two to begin."

"Turning Frère Léon loose on this project may have been a gross mistake," Paul said, winking at Solange. "He seems to think he runs the place now."

"I do, when you're off trotting to wherever it is you go. And it's a good thing that I do, because someone needs to be in charge, especially since you're spending so much more time up at The Mission these days."

The Mission had been rebuilt for six months now, with a nice-sized annexe to the infirmary. There were four properly supplied hospital rooms instead of one, besides the actual infirmary area, which had been enlarged. It had been Solange's father's donation to the cause since he'd given up on the idea of getting his daughter into a medical setting of his choice. He still didn't know that she would never bear him a grandson, but Solaina was pregnant now, and his frequent trips to visit her in Dharavaj seemed to make him forget all about Solange. For now. In time, she would probably tell him. When she and Paul were ready.

"As I seem to recall, you were the one who started all this," Solange teased Frère Léon. "*All* of this."

"And that part of my work is done." He glanced at the plain gold band on Solange's left hand, smiling. "Although you didn't make it easy on me."

"Well, let me make it just a bit tougher on *you*," Paul interjected. "I have a potential donor coming here to Abbeville in the morning. He's interested in contributing to the children's ward. Contributing substantially. And he wants to take a look at the hospital. But I'll be up at The Mission with my wife, helping her handle the next clinic day. Meaning guess who's going to be wining, dining and convincing the donor to give generously?" Frère Léon's ankle was healing nicely, but it wouldn't take him to the mountain again. In spite of it, he was settling in happily at the hospital, and Paul was turning over more and more of the administrative duties to him, including some of the fundraising aspects. Which turned out to be a wonderful match because both the good brother and the hospital were thriving. For Paul, it was a win-win situation. And the bonus was more time with Solange.

A broad grin crossed Frère Léon's face. "And I have just the thing I believe will work on him. In fact, I'll bet that by the time he leaves, his contribution will have doubled. Have a good trip. See you when you get back." Frère Léon gave Solange an affectionate peck on the cheek then bounced, slightly off-kilter now, out of the office, planing his next venture.

"I didn't bring the truck down with me this time," Solange said, smiling.

"That's OK. We can take mine up to Ambrose."

She shook her head. "I think it's time to introduce you to the *tap-tap*. And if we hurry, we'll have just enough time for me to give you proper instruction before the next one comes by the hospital."

"Proper instruction on how to ride the *tap-tap*? That wouldn't, by chance, have anything to do with making me ride up on top with the other men?" Paul asked.

Solange shook her head, then grabbed him by the hand. "No. The only proper instruction you'll be getting from me is on how a husband and wife can pass the time while waiting for the next *tap-tap* to come by." She arched her eyebrows suggestively. "Or the one after that, depending on how that wait turns out. And who knows? Maybe you'll even grow to love the *tap-tap*."

"Maybe I already am." Paul pulled Solange into his arms and lowered his lips to hers.

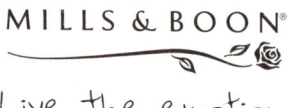

Live the emotion

DECEMBER 2005 HARDBACK TITLES

ROMANCE™

Title	Author	Code	ISBN
The High-Society Wife	Helen Bianchin	H6292	0 263 18787 X
The Virgin's Seduction	Anne Mather	H6293	0 263 18788 8
Traded to the Sheikh	Emma Darcy	H6294	0 263 18789 6
The Italian's Pregnant Mistress	Cathy Williams	H6295	0 263 18790 X
For Revenge...Or Pleasure?	Trish Morey	H6296	0 263 18791 8
The Greek's Bridal Bargain	Melanie Milburne	H6297	0 263 18792 6
Her Tycoon Protector	Amanda Browning	H6298	0 263 18793 4
Bought by a Billionaire	Kay Thorpe	H6299	0 263 18794 2
Father by Choice	Rebecca Winters	H6300	0 263 18795 0
Princess of Convenience	Marion Lennox	H6301	0 263 18796 9
A Husband To Belong To	Susan Fox	H6302	0 263 18797 7
Having the Boss's Babies	Barbara Hannay	H6303	0 263 18798 5
Betrothed to the Prince	Raye Morgan	H6304	0 263 18799 3
The Least Likely Groom	Linda Goodnight	H6305	0 263 18800 0
Needed: Full-time Father	Carol Marinelli	H6306	0 263 18801 9
Sheikh Surgeon	Meredith Webber	H6307	0 263 18802 7

HISTORICAL ROMANCE™

Title	Author	Code	ISBN
The Officer and the Lady	Dorothy Elbury	H618	0 263 18825 6
The Rake's Revenge	Gail Ranstrom	H619	0 263 18826 4
Ransom Bride	Anne Herries	H620	0 263 18952 X

MEDICAL ROMANCE™

Title	Author	Code	ISBN
The Surgeon's Engagement Wish	Alison Roberts	M531	0 263 18849 3
The Doctor's Courageous Bride	Dianne Drake	M532	0 263 18850 7

Live the emotion

DECEMBER 2005 LARGE PRINT TITLES

ROMANCE™

The Greek's Bought Wife *Helen Bianchin*	1823	0 263 18603 2
Bedding His Virgin Mistress *Penny Jordan*	1824	0 263 18604 0
His Wedding-Night Heir *Sara Craven*	1825	0 263 18605 9
The Sicilian's Defiant Mistress *Jane Porter*	1826	0 263 18606 7
The Outback Engagement *Margaret Way*	1827	0 263 18607 5
Rescued by a Millionaire *Marion Lennox*	1828	0 263 18608 3
A Family To Belong To *Natasha Oakley*	1829	0 263 18609 1
Parents of Convenience *Jennie Adams*	1830	0 263 18610 5

HISTORICAL ROMANCE™

The Disgraced Marchioness *Anne O'Brien*	316	0 263 18513 3
Her Knight Protector *Anne Herries*	317	0 263 18514 1
Lady Lyte's Little Secret *Deborah Hale*	318	0 263 18957 0

MEDICAL ROMANCE™

The Doctor's Special Touch *Marion Lennox*	585	0 263 18487 0
Crisis at Katoomba Hospital *Lucy Clark*	586	0 263 18488 9
Their Very Special Marriage *Kate Hardy*	587	0 263 18489 7
The Heart Surgeon's Proposal *Meredith Webber*	588	0 263 18490 0

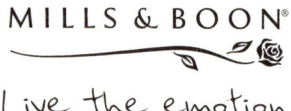

Live the emotion

JANUARY 2006 HARDBACK TITLES

ROMANCE™

Title	Author	Code	ISBN
The Italian Duke's Wife	Penny Jordan	H6308	0 263 19102 8
Shackled by Diamonds	Julia James	H6309	0 263 19103 6
Bought by her Husband	Sharon Kendrick	H6310	0 263 19104 4
The Royal Marriage	Fiona Hood-Stewart	H6311	0 263 19105 2
The Desert Virgin	Sandra Marton	H6312	0 263 19106 0
At the Cattleman's Command	Lindsay Armstrong	H6313	0 263 19107 9
The Millionaire's Runaway Bride	Catherine George	H6314	0 263 19108 7
His Secretary Mistress	Chantelle Shaw	H6315	0 263 19109 5
The Wedding Arrangement	Lucy Gordon	H6316	0 263 19110 9
His Inherited Wife	Barbara McMahon	H6317	0 263 19111 7
Marriage Reunited	Jessica Hart	H6318	0 263 19112 5
O'Reilly's Bride	Trish Wylie	H6319	0 263 19113 3
Counterfeit Princess	Raye Morgan	H6320	0 263 19114 1
Newborn Daddy	Judy Christenberry	H6321	0 263 19115 X
High-Altitude Doctor	Sarah Morgan	H6322	0 263 19116 8
The Surgeon's Pregnancy Surprise	Laura MacDonald	H6323	0 263 19117 6

HISTORICAL ROMANCE™

Title	Author	Code	ISBN
The Enigmatic Rake	Anne O'Brien	H621	0 263 19030 7
The Silver Lord	Miranda Jarrett	H622	0 263 19031 5
His Duty, Her Destiny	Juliet Landon	H623	0 263 19032 3

MEDICAL ROMANCE™

Title	Author	Code	ISBN
His Secret Love-Child	Marion Lennox	M533	0 263 19078 1
Her Honourable Playboy	Kate Hardy	M534	0 263 19079 X

1205 Gen Std HB

JANUARY 2006 LARGE PRINT TITLES

ROMANCE™

The Ramirez Bride *Emma Darcy*	1831	0 263 18923 6
Exposed: The Sheikh's Mistress *Sharon Kendrick*	1832	0 263 18924 4
The Sicilian Marriage *Sandra Marton*	1833	0 263 18925 2
At the French Baron's Bidding *Fiona Hood-Stewart*	1834	0 263 18926 0
Their New-Found Family *Rebecca Winters*	1835	0 263 18927 9
The Billionaire's Bride *Jackie Braun*	1836	0 263 18928 7
Contracted: Corporate Wife *Jessica Hart*	1837	0 263 18929 5
Impossibly Pregnant *Nicola Marsh*	1838	0 263 18930 9

HISTORICAL ROMANCE™

Betrayed and Betrothed *Anne Ashley*	319	0 263 18899 X
The Abducted Heiress *Claire Thornton*	320	0 263 18900 7
Marrying Miss Hemingford *Mary Nichols*	321	0 263 19066 8

MEDICAL ROMANCE™

The Celebrity Doctor's Proposal *Sarah Morgan*	589	0 263 18851 5
Undercover at City Hospital *Carol Marinelli*	590	0 263 18852 3
A Mother for His Family *Alison Roberts*	591	0 263 18853 1
A Special Kind of Caring *Jennifer Taylor*	592	0 263 18854 X